BEWITCHED BEGINNINGS

A PARANORMAL WOMEN'S FICTION NOVEL

MIDLIFE STRIKES
BOOK ONE

MARA WEBB

PROLOGUE

SUNDAY MORNING

The crime scene tape flapped in the wind, sounding almost like machine gun fire as the ocean breeze rolled across from the shore. All I could manage to do was stare forward, the sound of a voice in my right ear almost blurring into the background. I couldn't hear the words they were saying, the shock was too much.

A small crowd had gathered, some of them pulling out phones to document the gurney being rolled along the sidewalk. *'Say something, Tess.'* I wasn't sure if it was my own subconscious speaking, or the strange voice that had been following me for days.

The salty air of my hometown provided little comfort as I caught sight of the gurney approach the ambulance doors, the body on top of it completely covered in a white sheet. There was a dead person under there.

When I'd been a nurse it was perfectly normal to see dead people, an occupational hazard. Not a job for the squeamish, nursing. But I didn't work at the hospital anymore, and as the ambulance doors closed I felt my heart thumping in my chest. Was I about to have a panic attack?

"Do you understand what I'm saying to you? We need you to come in for questioning, Ms. Chase," the officer repeated. The voice came into focus and I turned to see the uniformed man beside me.

"Am I under arrest?" I asked.

CHAPTER 1

FIVE DAYS EARLIER

I have passed the bakery on Barksdale Drive every day for the last twenty-five years, always before the doors open for customers. I'm an early riser, as soon as my eyes are open I get out of bed and start the day. Although the speed in which I can physically get up has slowed recently.

Once out of bed I stretch my arms up as if reaching for the ceiling, loosening the muscles around my spine in preparation for another day of work. One advantage of living alone is that everything is always exactly where I last left it, so I find my bathroom in pristine condition without a single damp towel on the floor or shaved beard whiskers in the sink.

It means I am able to launch into my routine without delay, taming my bedhead, washing my face, applying serums and creams to counter father time's effect on my skin and finally a generous application of sunscreen before heading downstairs. I throw on a pair of slightly torn jeans and a t-shirt, no need to dress up for the day I have planned and make for the kitchen.

I grab a Tupperware box from the fridge with a breakfast I prepared the day before – a new habit I'm trying to develop – and throw it in a tote bag before heading outside. The street is quiet, as it always is, and I set off without having to drag out a goodbye or announce when I'll be home – a *disadvantage* of living alone.

For a variety of reasons I had been drawn to the idea of working through my bucket list over the past twelve months, tackling all manner of activities in the name of living life to its fullest. In hindsight, running a half-marathon was a stupid idea. Not stupid, that's not the right word. The running itself wasn't the problem, it was the shallow pothole my right foot fell into around mile nine. My ankle hadn't been the same since.

Summer mornings could be deceptively cool, the dew on the grass mixed with the chill of the air blowing over the ocean made the entire harbor town feel as if we had a cold day ahead. Five hours from now there would be a line around the block for the ice cream parlor and folks would be desperately seeking shade.

Kettle Harbor was a sea-side town that felt isolated on account of a national park separating us from the rest of the country on one side, and an ocean on the other. I continued along Barksdale Drive, turning left onto Bridge Street and then heading in the direction of the beach.

I used to run through town in my twenties, even in my early thirties I'd tried to keep on top of my physical health. The daily runs became every-other-day runs, then I would replace one of the runs with a yoga class. It was a slippery slope to get to where I was now, it hadn't happened overnight. Divorce has a way of making you re-evaluate your priorities, so now I was back to daily walks with a view to jogging in the near future.

I still planned to blame the ankle pain for a few more weeks though.

The briny air intensified as I got closer to the coast, a scent as comforting as grandma's Christmas cookies, or fresh bed sheets.

"Good morning, Tess!" a male voice bellowed from a boat deck. I gave a wave to Scott Edwards, the owner and operator of *the* whale spotting tour. Many other companies had come and gone, but his was the one that lasted. Over the years he had acquired all manner of equipment to track whales in the water so that he was able to guarantee a sighting (or your money back!).

I crossed over to the other sidewalk and got close enough to Scott's boat that I could see what he was doing. He had three squares of fabric in his hands and was holding them up against the logo of 'Whale Watch'.

"Are you planning to upholster the outside of the boat? I don't know much about sailing, but that sounds like a bad idea to me," I joked.

"Looking to upgrade the seats inside, I got these swatches on the internet, and I've been staring at them for two days," he replied.

"What's wrong with the chairs as they are?"

"The pattern has faded in the sun and a few of the chairs have tears in them..." he said, swapping out the dark blue square with white polka dots for one that was also dark blue but with thin white tree branches. "I've been advised to make the *inside* of the boat more 'photograph-friendly', which is why I'm doing it now. If I'm doing my job right them people are taking pictures of the whales in the water, though. It seems like a waste of time *and* money."

"Maybe you should get your advice from elsewhere," I smiled.

"It's my sister, she's the one with all the wild ideas," he shrugged, raising a hand to give a stiff wave to the 'Whale Watch' office building where his sister, Lisa, worked. Scott wanted to be out on the water as much as possible, and Lisa preferred dry land. She was more than happy to take care of all the admin, a woman that had her day planned down to the minute.

Lisa the clock watcher, and Scott the whale lover – Whale Watch. Lisa moved in the window of the sea-view office and then quickly turned her attention back to her computer.

"Are you in a rush?" I asked.

"She's booked in the guys to come and recover all the seats at the end of next week. I have to make a decision today or we won't be able to order the fabric in time and there's a cancellation fee. Do you see her out here looking at fabric squares? Of course not. You'd think she was allergic to the water the way she stays in there."

"Doesn't she get seasick?" I asked.

"Yeah, but still..." he sighed, turning to look out over the glistening water. The few whisps of cloud overhead were pierced by dazzling beams of golden sunshine, the entire ocean veneered in a diamond sheen that blinded. "There's no place I'd rather be than out there."

"And I'd love to stay here and look at his view, too, but I've got places to be."

"Busy day at the hotel?" he said, hopping down off the deck to join me on land.

Hotel. I almost laughed at the word. I, Theresa Chase, owned a hotel on the sea front of my hometown. A gift from my late grand-mother in her will, although that's using the word 'gift' generously in my opinion. It had been on its last legs ten years ago, so you can only imagine the state of it when I took over.

I'd lost my husband and my grandmother within weeks of each other. My grandmother was now in the place that we go to after life on earth, and my husband was now in the bed of a twenty-nine-year-old nursing assistant with a lower back tattoo. Correction, she was in *my* bed as I gave up the house in the divorce.

Gran gave me the hotel and I must have had the keys in my possession for weeks before I even dared visit the place. Months on and I still hadn't explored every room, it was a huge building that was in desperate need of some work, fortunately the inheritance had also included a good chunk of cash that was facilitating the renovations.

It bewildered me as to why she hadn't upgraded the place herself, she had money to pay for it all. It was as if she was always intending to pass the buck to someone else. Why not my sister? Oh, because she has a job in the police department, and it would be too much to load on her plate.

"Yeah, still on for this weekend," I said, my pulse beginning to pound in my temples as I considered the fact that I was officially re-opening in just a few days. I'd never owned a hotel before, never so much as taken one business class at college, and now here I was about to throw myself in at the deep end.

I'd been a nurse for many years, my husband and I actually met as students, and he put a ring on my finger the night we graduated. At the time it seemed like a great idea to marry a doctor, wasn't that supposed to come with financial stability and luxury vacations? I half-thought we might have our own boat out on the marina after a few years practicing medicine.

We were like ships in the night most of the time. Working at the same hospital on opposite shifts meant that we didn't see each other at work or at home. Little-miss lower back tattoo strategically re-arranged her work schedule to get as much face-to-face time with him as possible, and now they're together and I'm stood staring out to sea alone at seven o'clock in the morning.

There was no time to dwell on that now, I had work to do.

I said goodbye to Scott and continued along Bridge Street until I came to the sign for 'Moody Moon', the oddly named hotel that now bore my name as its owner. Could I have changed the name to some-thing a little less obscure? Was there time for that before opening? Probably not.

The tide was low, the beach was empty apart from a dog walker or two and I stared over at Kettle Island. It was one mile away from the mainland, accessible by pedestrians at low tide via a raised area of land that was known as Kettle Bridge. An aerial view of the harbor would show that the mainland looked a little like a cupped hand preparing to catch a baseball – the island being the ball in this anal-ogy, obviously.

The island is uninhabited. It has a number of high points that provide phenomenal views of the water and occasionally you can get lucky enough to see the whales offshore. Have tourists tried to drive over there at low tide? Of course. Have some been silly enough to *park* on Kettle Bridge only to finish their hike and come back to find their car submerged in water? Absolutely.

Tide Charts are posted everywhere, I'm quite sure there's an app for it now too.

I followed Bridge Street around the curve of the mainland, hugging the beach all the way, and found myself passing Shaded Wood, a care facility a few hundred yards away from Moody Moon. I wouldn't bother him at this hour, but I would make sure to visit today. The benches that sat in a line along the lawn looked tempting as the pain in my right ankle started to throb, but I'd have to walk it off.

I continued on towards the hotel, emptied the mailbox, and let myself inside. I would need to savor the quiet for a few minutes before I'd need to get started with my day's projects.

The reception area was something I was incredibly proud of. When I'd first been here after getting the keys, it had been fitted with a stained carpet, damp spots raising from the corners of the room and strange sun-bleached patches where paintings on the walls had been moved and never replaced. I'd ripped up the dirty carpet as a matter of priority, had someone address the damp issue, and stripped the wallpaper.

The floor was now a checkerboard of white and black tiles, the walls painted an immaculate white and adorned with black framed photographs of the harbor. I wanted guests to get the right impression when they came here, this was a clean establishment. In a way it was much like my own home at this point; in total order simply because I was the only one in it.

I ran a finger along the wooden reception desk, not a speck of dust to be found. I continued on towards the staff area where I would eat my breakfast and then head out back to inspect the courtyard – the fancy name I had chosen to give the paved area at the back of the building that surrounded the pool.

I opened my Tupperware box, inspected the wrapped bagel and fruits I'd packed up yesterday, and then sat down at the small dining table to eat. I glanced at the mail one by one; coupon for something I didn't want, flyer for an event that had already happened, phone bill, and then…

An invitation to a party that made it hard to swallow, for a second I thought I might choke on the mouthful of bagel I had been enjoying but I somehow managed to regain control of myself. I stared at the names and felt angry, sad tears swelling in each eye. My ex-husband had not only gotten engaged to little-miss lower back tattoo but had the gall to invite me to the engagement party to celebrate the occasion. I quickly lost my appetite.

CHAPTER 2

$\mathcal{I}$ dragged the pressure washer out of the storage shed and stopped by the outdoor faucet, surveying the discolored stone around the pool area. The pool had been drained weeks ago and the next phase was to have the tiles inside it cleaned out. I had outsourced the job, the thought of carrying machinery up and down the ladder with my ankle in its current state was enough to encourage me to pay someone else to do it.

Engaged. A flashbulb memory of the invitation struck me and caused an acidic taste to rise up in my mouth. I attached the faucet to the pressure washer, and began blasting green slime off the closest patch of concrete, muttering to myself all the while.

"We were dating for two years before he proposed to me, two *years,*" I ranted. "What a stupid man. What a stupid, stupid man. Why would I want front row seats to him groping a woman half his age? Maybe I *will* show up, maybe I'll—"

"Everything alright?" a voice hollered. I shut off the pressure washer and noticed Lena trying to clamber over the fence. "The front door was locked and so were the gates and you weren't answering your cell!"

"Sorry, I totally forgot you said you were coming," I said, rushing over to the gate closest to her, pulling a set of keys out of my pockets and releasing the padlock. "Get down from there, you'll have your hands full of splinters! The locks are more for show than anything. If you shoulder charge it even a little it opens. I need to get new ones."

She dropped down and walked through the gate, inspecting her palms for foreign objects; she'd gotten lucky, so turned her attention back to me. She had a sympathetic look on her face, a half-smile that was pulled upwards as she crinkled her nose, I'd known her well enough to know that expression. It meant, *'have you heard what's happened?'*

"Did he invite you too?" I asked.

"I got it this morning, I almost choked on my cereal," she replied. "Tess, I think we need to arrange an intervention for that poor girl."

"How have you managed to find a way to feel sorry for *her* in this situation?" I said, raising an eyebrow.

"I think he's got his hooks in, you know how he is."

"Yes I do, I know all too well!" I looked back at the bench behind me and considered whether I was willing to sit down on something so filthy. The reason I'd worn this outfit today was because I anticipated getting dirty, so sat down anyway. "I left the hospital because I couldn't deal with seeing either of them anymore, I've got this place now and I was quite happy trying to put it all behind me but—"

"You were married for a long time, Tess. It was never going to be all that easy," she said, sitting down beside me.

"I trained her, you know. When she first started I helped her navigate the hospital… urgh, she's just… I don't even know who to be angry at. If I don't try to make a life for myself then I'm going to stay trapped in the one I had with him and it doesn't exist anymore."

We both stared out across the dirt covered pool area, watching the patch I'd already blasted begin to dry in the sun. I had to employ a great deal of imagination where this hotel was concerned, try to utilize hope wherever possible that this place could be a thing of beauty if I just persevered with the renovations. The pool area was probably the one place that needed cleaning and nothing else, this side of the hotel had managed to avoid my grandmother's questionable décor choices.

"Have you seen her this week?" Lena asked.

"Still avoiding. What you don't know can't hurt you, that's what I figured," I nodded.

Casey – aka little-miss lower back tattoo – had decided to leave her position at the hospital almost two months ago in pursuit of a career in private care. I was well aware that the hours were more predictable and that the money could be just as good, especially for a qualified nurse, but given that she'd been such an enthusiastic employee at the hospital I figured she'd happily stay put.

Well, you can only *imagine* my delight when I strolled into Shaded Wood care home to visit my father one day and saw that they'd brought on a new recruit. She worked in the very place my dad lived, I'd left the hospital in the hopes of avoiding them forever – a mature approach to it all, I'm sure you agree – and then she made herself *almost* unavoidable.

I say almost because I call at the beginning of every week when the schedule is made and ask when she will be on shift and when she won't. That is now what dictates my visits to my own dad. I appreciate that it's not sustainable, but for now it seems to be working. Sort of.

"I didn't read the whole invite, I thought actual steam was going to start firing out of both ears," I said. "Where is it?"

"O'Malley's," she replied, bracing herself for a response. My ex-husband has selected the one bar in town that happened to host our own engagement party over twenty years earlier. The acidic taste rose up in my mouth once again. "Maybe he just forgot?"

"So he forgot but you remembered?" I said. "Why would he invite me to that? He's only done it to make sure that I haven't avoided the news, right? I don't understand how he went from being this man that I was in love with to someone that hurts me for sport."

"Jack was always a son of a bi—" Lena began, but I raised an index finger to cut her off.

"Don't!" I looked around nervously, bracing myself for something to happen in response to the casual use of a curse word. I wasn't nuts, but I could swear this place could *hear* me. Even if I swore under my breath something would fall over or shatter. I was certain.

"Not this, still," she tutted, rolling her eyes. "I think you need to call the number I gave you. I started seeing this therapist after Ben passed and he's been really helpful."

Ben. Lena's husband had left her in a different way, he'd suffered a heart attack one night when Lena was working a night shift at the hospital. Part of the reason she had started seeing a therapist had been to help her tackle the guilt she'd felt about not being there when it happened, not being able to help him in his hour of need.

Here I was complaining that Jack had ended our marriage to shack up with a younger model, and Lena was still working through the grief that comes with losing a man that didn't want to leave. I know everyone has their problems, if you start comparing your situations to other people's then you'll always find someone that has it worse than you.

"I'll call, I will. I feel like I'm still reacting to it like it just happened, but apparently enough time has passed that he's making wedding plans so... well maybe it's my cue to put myself out there," I shrugged.

"I'm going to dare you to do something," she said, wickedly.

"No, no dares. I'm a business owner now, I can't be busting my ass climbing onto the roof days before this place opens."

"Excuse me, I have only dared you to climb onto a roof *once*, and that was years ago!"

"Yeah, but weirdly it's always the one that sticks out in my memory," I grinned.

"If you hadn't fallen off it, that night would have been completely un-memorable," she replied. We were all grateful for the overgrown hedges at the side of my parent's house that night, they provided a cushioned – if somewhat spiky – place to land. "Anyway, I was planning on daring you to do something brave that doesn't require any physical danger."

"We're supposed to be cleaning up the pool area, I've got a guy coming here tomorrow to—"

"Invite someone to the grand opening, someone that you have your eye on. There has to be someone, right? It's risk free! You're already throwing a party, there'd be enough people there that you don't have to think about spending one on one time with them and—"

"Lena, you said no physical danger," I huffed. "This feels dangerous to me. I've never… Jack can…"

"Say it," she demanded.

"Men get better looking with age, isn't that what everyone says? I married a man when I was at my prime, and then the prime years came and went and then he's tossed me out like old trash to move on with a wrinkle-free, smooth skinned, pretty little thing that doesn't have to worry about night sweats and sagging jowls."

"You're really going to stand there and tell me you think you're passed it? I am two months older than you, young lady, so if you think *you're* too old to be desired ever again then what exactly do you think will happen to me? Should I just crawl into a coffin now and wait for the inevitable?" she said, raising to her feet mid-speech to emphasize her annoyance.

"No but—"

"Ben has been dead for eighteen months, and my relationship status has *nothing* to do with how I feel about my appearance. The most adventurous thing you've done in the last year has been bust your ankle running a marathon, and when the joint has had enough time to heal then you can get back out there and keep running. Are you picking up on this analogy, Tess? Because I feel like it's a good one."

"You want me to get my sneakers back on," I sighed. She was right, she was always right. Lena and Ben had travelled, they'd been bold and curious about the world and I'd always envied the freedom they gave themselves to get out there and do new things. Lena was a nurse, just like I'd been, and Ben had been a teacher. They used his long school breaks to visit Europe and Asia, always coming home with fascinating accounts of their time abroad that always caused a tension in the pit of my stomach.

Jack and I hadn't been that couple. We'd never really been

anywhere, only ever vacationing somewhere within driving distance. We never even travelled far enough for the accents to change. I had a freedom now that I'd never had, I was hurtling towards fifty at an alarming speed but it was like my life was starting over.

I could go anywhere I wanted, spend my evenings doing whatever I liked, and yes, maybe even flirt with the idea of dating again. Well, maybe not just yet. I had a business to open this Friday and if my life was starting again then it would be appropriate to take baby steps.

Lena grabbed the pressure washer from me and began blasting filth off the ground, leaving me on the bench to ponder my next move. I flexed my right ankle and noted that it felt easier to move than it had done even a week ago, perhaps it truly was time to start running again.

CHAPTER 3

*L*ena and I were now wearing half the dirt that we'd liberated from the pool area, but it was nothing a washing machine and a quick shower couldn't fix. Once the pool was cleaned out and refilled this place would be ready to go. The new furniture was waiting in the storage shed and would be unwrapped and assembled as the final act of the hotel renovations.

I felt proud of what I'd accomplished, it had been months of negotiations with local contractors, budget adjustments, and bottles of chardonnay, but it was finally coming to an end. All that was left now was the actual 'running a hotel' part, which arguably was the greater challenge.

I'd obtained every license and qualification, ticked every box with regards to the legal side of things, and had even managed to recruit two staff members to help me out with the reception desk, Lena's niece Molly and a boy was the son of a man Scott owed a favor too. Apparently by me offering this young man employment, Scott had paid his debt. I assumed it was something to do with gambling and hadn't asked too many questions.

"What are you doing with the rest of the day?" Lena asked, glancing at her watch, "well, what's left of it."

"Visiting dad," I replied.

"I take it Casey isn't working today then," she said, flopping down onto the bench.

"She finished at three, so the coast should be clear," I smiled, sitting next to her.

"Don't the management find it weird that you're basically stalking a young staff member?"

"There was no need for you to add in the word 'young', and it's hardly stalking. It's the *opposite* of stalking, I'm specifically asking when she won't be in so I can visit in peace."

"Right... but I still think they shouldn't be giving out that information. You could be an axe-murdering psychopath for all they know! You could be waiting for her to get off shift so you can follow her into an alley and—"

"They know it's me, Lena, they know I'm not trying to plan an assassination," I laughed. The mirth was short-lived, I felt a sudden weight on my shoulders as I realized that what I was doing was kicking the can down the road. I couldn't avoid her forever, they'd sent an invitation to the hotel for crying out loud. Neither of them had any intention of letting me pretend they didn't exist, so I'd have to come up with a better coping strategy at some point.

"We can make a plan for Saturday night, how about box wine on the island? We can do one of those cleansing ceremonies where we burn all the pictures you have of Jack and, you know, release him to the universe," she suggested, her eyes twinkling with excitement as the prospect.

"Jack isn't the one that needs releasing, it's me. But maybe setting his stuff on fire would help with that, so I'm in. Scott can pick us up if we stay over there too long, we might have to wade out a little into the shallows but I'd rather get the bottom of my jeans wet than be within a mile of O'Malley's."

"It's a date," Lena nodded, then furrowing her brow. "I've got to ask, and I know you've told me but I forget, did you say you have guests booked in from opening night? Are you even free on Saturday?"

"Yes, the first bookable night is *next* Friday, not this weekend. I needed to get the hotel up to standard and have it inspected, *and* I need to get through the training for Molly and Lewis before we have anyone through the doors properly. We actually have a few people booked in already so I'm praying nothing goes wrong with the inspection because otherwise I'm going to have to make some very uncomfortable phone calls."

"Everything will be just fine," she assured me. "Go and see your dad, call me when you get home, and put some thought into which fine young man you'll be luring to the hotel opening."

"Young?"

"If Jack Stevens can bag himself a twenty-nine year old, then so can you!"

"I appreciate the sentiment, but I think that's a bit too close to cradle-robbing in my opinion. Besides, where exactly is it that you think I can pick up a man? I'm either here, at home, or at the care home. Do you want me to start hitting on some of my dad's elderly friends? Maybe I could start passing out my number to the care workers there so that every subsequent visit is so awkward that I can't go there anymore. Is that what you want? For my father to lose out on his visits because—"

"Tess," she said, giving me *the look*. "You don't need to find 'the one' on your first try, but find *someone*."

With that, she patted me affectionately on the shoulder and headed out of the unlocked gate towards her car. She'd successfully kept me distracted the entire day, but now I was left with the most dangerous feeling of all. Hope. As I packed away the pressure washer, locked the gate, and headed inside to utilize one of the showers, I found myself wondering if it was really possible for me to make the second half of my life the 'better' half.

I didn't need that to involve a man, I just needed it to involve possibilities. I could shape my life into whatever suited me best, I could make myself the priority now, I was free to say 'yes' and 'no' without consulting another living soul first.

Obviously I was still a daughter, and a sister, and a business owner, and a friend. I couldn't exactly pack a suitcase and drop off the face of the planet. I showered quickly, threw on a dress that I'd left here in case I ever needed a quick change, and also grabbed my coat. Apparently my hormones had decided that now was a good time to swing my body temperature in the opposite direction and I was freezing.

It would only last a few minutes, I'd probably be taking the coat off again before I walked through the doors of Shaded Wood, but at least I'd be vaguely comfortable until it ended.

I stepped into the day room and scanned the place for my dad's face. He'd been wheeled over to a large window that gave a view over the gardens at the back, he had an old radio on his lap that he had tuned in to a station that played classical music.

I was wearing my 'visitor' badge, dutifully, and as I crossed the floor I offered a curtesy nod to each staff member I passed. One of the people that nodded back was *not* a staff member, but was however completely naked. As a nurse I'd seen more than my fair share of nudity, but to have a man in his late eighties do it in the middle of the day room of a care home was something else.

Dad's physiotherapist, Chris, was escorting another resident off to a treatment room and gave me a smile when he saw me, stopping in his tracks as if he planned to say something, then turned to the nude man in front of me. He was holding the handles of a wheelchair and looked around for backup.

"Lionel, do you remember what we said about wearing clothes?" he asked. "The last time we had a conversation about it you agreed that you were going to keep them on when you were in the community spaces."

Lionel looked down and gasped, as if his own nakedness had caught him off guard. "And I've said to you that you have to keep your plums at room temperature, it says so in the Reader's Digest!"

"There were talking about actual plums though, remember?" Chris said, reaching for a blanket that was draped over the back of one of the chairs nearby and handing it to the elderly resident.

"I'm not ashamed of my body! You can't tell me how to live!" Lionel yelled. He took the blanket out of Chris's hands, threw it across the room, then turned to run away. I was treated to a front row seat to Lionel's plums as he tried to sprint away from the staff that were now trying to heard him like a wild animal. It would have been a great time for the Benny Hill theme tune to start playing.

Chris was still holding on to a wheelchair that was occupied by another elderly gentleman, this one was completely dressed and seemingly unphased by what appeared to be a regular occurrence.

"Louise? Could you help Ron to the therapy suite? I just want to have a quick word with Ms. Chase," he said, beckoning over a woman that had been quite happily indulging in a crossword behind the nurse's station desk. She brought her puzzle book with her as she got up, looking directly at the elderly man in the wheelchair as she began to speak.

"Ron, I know you're a whizz with these things," she said, wrapping her palms around the handles of his chair, "I've been staring at this one clue for five minutes and I ain't got the first idea. It just says 'rowdy', that's the whole clue. The word is eight letters, and I know there ain't a word in the whole English language that you don't—"

Her voice trailed off as she rolled Ron along the corridor and out of sight. I turned to the physiotherapist, a man that insisted I refer to him as 'Chris' that had been working with my dad ever since the stroke. Apparently we'd all agreed not to mention the naked manhunt that was taking place beyond the windows – Lionel streaked across the back lawn, but I turned my attention back to the person in front of me.

"Good news? Bad news? Should I grab a Kleenex?" I said, anxiously.

"Tess, he took two steps today," Chris replied with a smile that reached his eyes.

"No, really? What? I don't—" I gasped, suddenly flustered and overwhelmed. I looked back over my shoulder to see dad by the window, clutching his radio.

"One of the nurses told him he'd be back on the dancefloor in no time, which I think is why he's listening to music over there. He's getting his rhythm back," he laughed. Before I realized what had happened, I'd thrown my arms around Chris and was hugging him, I felt reluctant hands embrace me before I peeled away.

"Sorry, I just… I can't believe it, thank you so much. Has he said anything?"

"Speech is not my area, but— no, I think he's doing really well with — I've never seen—" He stopped himself, as if trying to censor something.

"What were you about to say?" I asked. He shook his head. "You were going to say people don't completely lose their ability to speak, right?"

"It can be a little scrambled, but I've never worked with a patient that has fallen into silence like this."

I already knew it. I'd seen stroke patients at the hospital plenty of times, I knew that what my father was going through wasn't typical. I guess it was the elephant in the room that I was choosing to ignore. He should be speaking by now, but he wasn't. Was he doing it on purpose? That would be crazy, I shouldn't even entertain the idea. Yet…

"Look, your visits always put a smile on his face. I think that he's on the right road with his treatment and talking with him, asking him yes or no questions he can respond to… he likes hearing about your life, I can tell," Chris said. "Look, I've got to get going otherwise Louise is going to force Ron to finish that crossword for her. It was good to see you."

"Thanks, Chris," I replied. As he walked away down the corridor towards the treatment room I could hear Lena's words echoing in my ears and found my eyes wandering down to the physiotherapists rear end as he disappeared into a side room. Great, now I was a pervert. Just what I needed.

I pulled a chair over beside my dad and beamed at him as his eyes lit up. He turned off his radio and stretched out his arms for a hug. "Someone told me you could give Usain Bolt a run for his money," I teased.

He smiled proudly, but said nothing.

"You'll be glad to know that it looks like things might actually be done on time for the launch party. It would save me a few thousand dollars if *you* could come and sort the pool out for me though. Are you feeling up to it?" I teased. He shook his head with a grin. "Suit yourself. You know, I really thought your retirement would involve me taking advantage of your labor for free more often, this has been a real let down. Did you ever think about *me* before you had a stroke, dad? Huh?"

He laughed. If that was the only sound he was able to make in response to a conversation then that was just fine by me. A noise from the other side of the day room made us both look over to see what was going on.

A young man, maybe late twenties, was standing in the entrance holding a bouquet of flowers. That in and of itself was not a peculiar sight, but he was being yelled at by an elderly woman about ten feet to his left. Despite the heckling, he had his eyes fixed on something straight in front of him. It would appear that I had been mis-informed, as little-miss back tattoo *was* working tonight.

I could see the rock on her finger from here, the acidic taste in my mouth overwhelmed me and I almost turned away but for some reason I couldn't. The stranger in the doorway was trying to hand the flowers to her, and she was trying to refuse them. The elderly woman decided to hurl a handbag at the side of his head – *that* got his atten-tion – and as he was distracted, Casey scurried off into a staff-only area out of sight.

I turned back to dad who was giving me a sympathetic look. "Oh, don't look at me like that. I suppose you already knew about the engagement then, I bet she's been flashing that diamond to everyone."

Dad nodded. He lifted up two hands to mime using a steering wheel, pretending to pull out the keys from the imaginary ignition and then dragging the key through the air.

"You think I should key her car?" I laughed. He smiled in response. "Well, I'll keep it in mind. What would Michelle think of that though?"

He blew air out of his mouth with a *'pfft'* sound and swiped a dismissive hand at me. I knew that he meant, *'don't worry about what your sister would say.'*

"She already thinks I'm nuts, I don't need to add fuel to the fire," I said. He furrowed his brow for a second, then appeared to remember what it was I was talking about. "Yes, exactly. That's still happening by the way, I think we are up to nearly seven instances of it and she still thinks I'm making it up. She tried to tell me that a mind in shock can imagine all sorts of crazy things."

He raised a brow, as if to say, *'are you sure you're not crazy?'*

"If it had been once or twice then I'd ignore it dad. I'm telling you, that hotel is haunted."

He held up seven fingers, then gestured to the first finger on his left hand, he wanted me to run through each event. I think he quite liked my tales from the Moody Moon, he seemed to get a kick out of my stories and maybe he still thought I was just making them up to amuse him. But I wasn't, it was real. At least, it *seemed* real.

Lena thought I was out of my mind, Michelle explicitly told me to stop telling her ghost stories as she didn't like to hear about anything that might scare her – great quality for a cop, I'm sure you'll agree –, and dad? Well he loved it. So I started from the beginning and recounted every time I'd seen my grandmother's ghost.

CHAPTER 4

*J*couldn't sleep. I'd been staring at the ceiling above my bed for hours, hoping that I would eventually relax enough to drift off, but as I checked the time again I realized another forty-five minutes had past. It was now almost three o'clock in the morning. I started playing that stupid math game where I work out how many hours of sleep I would get if I fell asleep immediately.

I could hear a car turn onto the street, it drove past the house and carried on. At least I wasn't the only person awake. When should I admit defeat and turn on the light on my nightstand? Was it the hotel that was keeping my mind so alert? Maybe I was subconsciously more nervous about it than I'd wanted to admit. Or was it the engagement?

I turned on the light with a sigh and adjusted my pillows so I could sit up properly. I clasped my hands together and went to twist my wedding ring the way I usually did when I was looking to something to fidget with. It wasn't there. Even after months of not wearing it, I would find myself surprised by its absence. I'd taken it off and tucked it away. That band of gold had linked me to a person I was no longer linked to.

I couldn't help but think about the giant rock on Casey's finger.

I was hosting a launch party for the hotel *tonight*. The pool had been taken care of, the rooms were pristine, and the caterers had their instructions. I'd constructed a balloon arch with Lena's assistance, I had flowers being delivered mid-afternoon and I had my dress at the dry-cleaners ready for collection before the main event.

I didn't want to have bags under my eyes when I was thanking people for coming, I'd hoped to look like I had my life together. As I looked at the numbers on my watch tick over to three-thirty I knew it was too late to get the appropriate amount of 'beauty sleep', why did insomnia have to strike today of all days?

I'd had this launch party booked for weeks, I'd been telling people all around town and it had even been in the newspaper. Jack and Casey just *had* to throw an engagement party the same weekend, huh? There's no way that was a coincidence. He couldn't just let me move on with my life, he had to find these stupid ways to twist the knife. He ended our marriage, I don't know why he felt compelled to treat *me* like the deserter.

"Maybe I should key *his* car," I muttered.

Something sharp jabbed me in the shoulder, *"ow,"* I complained, turning to see if a feather had stabbed through the pillow case. At the foot of the bed I could see a whisp of smoke, barely visible in the dim light but enough to flood me with panic. *Fire.*

I tried to get out of bed but I couldn't move, I was held firm against the mattress as if paralyzed and my heart began pounding as I watched the smoke thicken. My eyes darted to the door, expecting to see grey clouds creeping beneath it from the hallway. Why wasn't the alarm going off? Why couldn't I move? The deep grey smoke was twirling like it was caught in a vortex, localized to one spot of my bedroom floor, growing almost silver and blue as the speed increased.

I'd read that hallucinations worsen during the menopause *if* the individual has a history of such psychotic symptoms – which I didn't. Was this how I found out I was completely mad? I struggled against my invisible restraints and willed my body to stop doing whatever *this* was. I was exhausted, stressed, anxious, heartbroken, and low on hormones. A horrific cocktail.

The twirling smoke slowed, then suddenly stopped. It hung like a tapestry in the air, a strange image of cloud that didn't move. The stillness was more alarming than the movement had been. I stared at it, afraid that it would suddenly move again but also unable to look away. Part of it projected forward slightly, like a hand pushing against a curtain, and a single word was spoken out into the night air that made my body shudder.

"Tess," the voice said. I blinked, opening my eyes to find the smoke had gone. Sunlight was flooding my bedroom, it was morning. I lifted up my left wrist, no longer paralyzed, and saw that it was seven o'clock, somehow the last three and a half hours had vanished in the blink of an eye and I was left wondering if I'd dreamt it all, or if I'd really just had my eighth encounter with my grandmother's spirit.

* * *

ONE SHOWER, a cup of coffee, and a bagel later, I was standing outside with my keys clutched in my hand looking at my hunk of junk car on the driveway. This garbage heap was the reason I walked so often, but considering all the tasks I needed to tick off before the launch party it was looking like the sensible choice. I could get from A to B quicker in this thing that on foot, theoretically.

This rust bucket was all I could afford. I had hopes that once the hotel was up and running with paying guests that I might be able to upgrade it, on the rare occasions that I did choose to drive somewhere it would splutter and lurch when I turned the key.

I looked at the list in my hand and tried to decide where I needed to get to first. I had to get to the dry cleaners, stop in to see my dad, call Michelle back because she'd left me two voicemail messages in the last two days and I hadn't gotten round to responding to them, check in at the hotel to make sure that the set up was on track, and speak to a reporter. Oh, and get my nails painted. Oh, and figure out how to do something with my hair because there would be pictures taken tonight.

I'd barely had three hours of sleep, I might have to grab another coffee while I was running errands. I unlocked the driver's side door, frowned at the cigarette burns on the fabric of the seat (a feature installed by a previous owner), and climbed inside.

I pulled out my phone and called Michelle, setting it to 'hands free' as it dialed so that I could start the engine. She picked up just as I was shouting, *'come on! Not today, come on!'* and punching the dashboard.

"Tess?" she answered. The car shuddered as the engine rattled to life and I let out a sigh of relief.

"Yeah, just in the car," I replied.

"I should buy you a bike, that thing you drive is a death trap. Every time we get a call about a traffic accident I assume it's you," she said.

"Why would you say that? You're jinxing me!" I laughed.

"To be honest when you missed my call the other day I figured the worst had happened."

"Yet you didn't come round to the house to check I was alive? Some sister you are," I teased, backing off the driveway cautiously and beginning to drive in the direction of the hotel.

"Did you listen to my voicemails? I was asking if you'd stopped in to see dad this week," she said.

"Yeah, have you?"

"Only once, it was a few days ago but I know his physio said he'd taken a step or something. Work's been a total nightmare and I couldn't get away. Is he coming tonight?" she asked.

"Who, dad or the physio?"

"Dad, obviously. I was thinking maybe I could wheel him over if he's up for it," she offered.

"I asked him the other day and he seemed interested but it's worth checking again. I'm planning to head over to see him in a minute so I can ask and let you know."

"You're planning to visit dad, first thing, on a weekday?" she gasped, faking astonishment. "What if *she's* there?!" Who needs enemies when you've got siblings, eh? "I… that was why I called you really, Tess. I heard about the, you know…"

"The engagement?" I guessed.

"He's a jerk, you know that, right? I know it's gotta sting but you are better off without him and if I wasn't a police officer I'd be tempted to hit him with my car."

"Thanks?" I laughed. "No need to murder anyone, but I appreciate the offer. I think. How did you hear about it?"

"I saw the rock on her finger when I was last there. She had this big dumb smile on her face as she was showing it off to the other staff and I knew you'd been trying to avoid being there when she was on shift so I figured you might not know about it yet."

I didn't want to tell her about the invite to the engagement party, I didn't even want to acknowledge that it was happening at all. I turned onto the parking lot behind Shaded Wood just as another call was coming through on my phone. "I'm going to have to love you and leave you because I think a reporter's trying to get hold of me," I explained.

"I'll see you tonight, text me about dad, okay?"

"Will do. Bye, Mich." I hit the 'end call and accept' button on my phone as I parked the car, and lifted the device to my ear while switching off 'hands free' mode. "Hello?"

"Theresa Chase?"

"The one and only," I replied. "Is this Gemma?"

"Yes, I'm glad I could get hold of you. I've had to swap my schedule around this morning, so would I be able to sit down with you this afternoon? I'd be free around three thirty. I can come to you, wherever you'll be."

I remembered the flower delivery, so suggested that she came to the hotel and met me there. My eye caught Casey's car in the parking lot as I ended the call. There was a single rose on the windscreen, the stem pinned against the glass by the wiper. Had Jack been here this morning? Irritation hit me as I tried to think of any time he'd done anything as romantic for me. I drew a blank.

I felt a cold shiver across my skin and noticed the hairs on my arm standing on end, a whisp of smoke appeared on the passenger side of the car and I wasn't sure what to be more concerned about; the possibility that it was another weird, paranormal encounter or that maybe my car was on fire. Either way, I got out in a hurry.

I made my way inside and quickly spotted my dad sitting by the TV watching a wildlife documentary. I didn't often visit at this time, or at least I hadn't recently. Casey was normally here, part of the reason she'd transferred to Shaded Wood was for the regular working hours that weren't an option at the hospital. Shift handover here was at six am and you could reasonably expect to work your eight hours and get out, nothing like the grueling fourteen hour days I had in my early nursing career.

I scanned the room for signs of her, like a small animal might look out for clues that a predator was close. I just wanted to speak to my dad quickly, check everything was alright, then get out of here without being noticed. The very last thing I wanted was to be trapped in an awkward conversation with Mrs. Stevens-to-be.

I managed to take two steps across the floor of the day room before I spotted her behind the nurses station. She was crying, explaining something to a male colleague who was nodding encouragingly, but there was an expression on his face that I couldn't quite read. He looked almost *angry*, as if she was telling him something he really didn't like.

He wrapped his arms around her and she sobbed against his shoulder, her face turned towards me but with her eyes closed as tears continued to roll down her cheeks. There was a bruise on her temple, a dark one that hadn't been there when I'd seen her a few days earlier. I caught sight of a bruise on her wrist, too.

Her friend squeezed her tightly in his embrace and I turned my attention back to my dad. She'd caught me staring, I was sure of it. She pulled the sleeve of her cardigan down to cover the marks on her wrist. I felt as if I'd seen something I shouldn't have.

CHAPTER 5

I was sat behind the reception desk when Gemma arrived. I'd been texting back and forth with Michelle about her bringing dad over later – he seemed enthusiastic about the prospect of getting out of the house – and I was now waiting on the flower delivery. Gemma stepped into the lobby with the kind of high heeled shoes that *click click* when you walk across hard floors.

She was a woman of enviable style, a blazer that matched her trousers and a smart shirt beneath made her look like she worked in a higher position that she actually did. The other reporters I'd encountered dressed in a much more casual manner, preferring jeans and t-shirt over a suit.

"Ms. Chase?" she said, extending a hand towards me.

"Yes, nice to see you again," I smiled, wondering if she would remember the time she interview me at the hospital about a fundraiser the nursing staff had organized a few years back. "Would you like a drink?"

"A glass of water would be perfect, I've been over on the island most of the morning and it's been a hot one," she said.

"Anything exciting happening over there?" I asked, retrieving a bottle of water from the fridge behind the reception desk and grabbing a clean glass.

"Another tourist group got stuck out there overnight, one of them tried to swim back to the mainland but they misjudged the strength of the current so the coast guard was called for a midnight rescue," she explained. "I think I was actually speaking with your sister."

"Michelle?"

"Yes," she said, taking the glass from my hand and inhaling half of the water in a few large gulps. "Thank you."

"What did she suggest? I don't know if the warning signs about the tide could be any bigger."

"Boats," she shrugged. "They're having an emergency phone line fitted that calls for a rescue, well at the minute the plan is that it goes straight through to Whale Watch because Scott offered to help out, but I don't think that's the long term plan. If people get stuck out on the island then he can head over to the shallows on the west side and they can wade to him for a ride back." I'd done that very thing on more than one occasion, I knew the spots on the island where I could get cellphone signal. "Anyway, I shouldn't bore you with all that! I came to talk about you!"

She pulled out a notepad and pen from her handbag and let her eyes wander over the reception area.

"I don't know if you ever saw the place when my grandmother owned it," I began. "She'd kept the same décor for decades, never updating the place. She said decorating was a messy job and she wanted to keep everything clean."

"Do you have any pictures of what it looked like before?" she asked.

"Yes, I kept them in a drawer back here," I replied, stepping back around the reception desk. "I haven't gotten around to it just yet, but I was thinking of hanging a few of these in the corridors. I was going to have them blown up, just the ones of the outside."

Gemma took the stack of photographs and began to look through them, stopping to inspect a picture of what the reception looked like before I'd renovated. She laughed, "I'm surprised the place stayed open if this was the first impression people got when they came in!"

There was a loud 'pop', then another. The balloon arch that Lena and I had constructed was still wobbling when I turned in the direction of the sound, a tiny whisp of smoke still swirling around it. An engine outside announced the arrival of the flower delivery van, I could see Stanley behind the wheel giving me a wave when he spotted me. "Sorry, I've just got to deal with that," I said, jerking my chin towards the doors.

"Of course. Do you mind if I...?" Gemma reached into her bag and pulled out a bag of potato chips.

"No, go right ahead," I replied, trying to mask my alarm that she was about to drop crumbs all over the floor.

By the time I was out front Stanley was already on his way into the building with the first giant bouquet of white flowers, "where do you want them?" he asked. The buttons on his shirt were under great strain around his stomach, and there was a light dusting of powdered sugar in the whiskers of his moustache. I didn't buy flowers all that often, in fact the last time Stanley had really had any business out of me was when I placed the order for my wedding bouquet.

"Just by the desk," I said, eyeing the vase in his hands. I stepped to the side of the doors to stare over at Kettle Island in all it's glory under the mid-afternoon sun. Even from here I could see folks laying out on blankets on it's sandy shore.

Hopefully the weather held for the rest of today and tomorrow, Lena had promised to keep me company over there for a few hours so that we could completely avoid the engagement party happening at O'Malley's.

"White flowers are for funerals, Theresa," a voice announced. I turned back towards the doors of the hotel to see who'd spoken, but both Gemma and Stanley were inside speaking with each other. I was alone outside.

"Hello?" I called out. No reply. Stanley carried three more white bouquets in vases to the reception area, then brought out a smaller bouquet and handed it to me directly. There were sunflowers, my favorite. "I didn't order these," I said.

"They have your address on the card," he replied, shrugging. "Maybe you have a secret admirer! I see a lot of anonymous senders in this line of work, I'm like cupid in a way. Love is good business for a florist, Tess! So whatever you've done to deserve these, keep it up!"

"Thanks, Stan," I mumbled, opening the small envelope attached to the stems in my hands. Anonymous sender? Hardly. Three little words were enough for me to figure it out, *good luck, Tessy.* There was only one person on earth that ever called me Tessy, and I'd divorced him.

* * *

THE HOURS that followed the flower delivery were tough. I'd driven the car from the Shaded Wood parking lot to my spot behind Moody Moon, which had given me a false confidence that it was going to be functional for the entire day. It had barely spluttered, there hadn't been a single back fire or scary rattling sound. As I'd driven along Bridge Street looking for a parking spot close to the dry-cleaners my luck ran out.

Looking for street parking here was always a nightmare given it's proximity to Kettle Bridge. I drove around the block looking for an empty space, but apparently there was a 'kids eat free' special at the lobster joint across the road from the laundry place. After my third lap of the block, I turned right on Center Street hoping that the next block over would somewhere I could pull over for a few minutes while I ran to grab my dress.

I turned again onto Cedar and spotted a gap in the row of cars along the edge of the sidewalk and immediately pulled into it. I checked the time on the dashboard clock, I had to be back at the hotel in two hours so I'd have to get a move on. I climbed out of the car and that's when I realized where I was. The panic of trying to find a place to park had clouded my sense of Kettle Harbor geography, and now I was stood a hundred yards down the street from O'Malley's.

I stared at the sign, the green clover and the name looking exactly as it had back when I was celebrating my own engagement there. There was a small alley that accessed a parking lot behind it, barely wide enough for a delivery truck to get through. I thought again of Jack's flowers and the note, a chill washed over me and I couldn't decide if it was from the horror that he was getting married again, or a hormone imbalance.

After triple checking that I had my ticket, I hurried around the corner along Center Street and ducked into the dry cleaners. The swarms of people outside the lobster restaurant across the road were talking loud enough that it was audible through the closed doors.

"Been like that all day," the woman behind the counter tutted. 'Catch of the Day', the seafood joint that was drawing in swarms of hungry customers, was famed for being the *cheapest* in town. Kettle Harbor had multiple seafood places, an inevitability in a coastal town, and everyone had strong opinions on how they ranked compared to each other.

I handed over my ticket and she sighed before sliding off the stool and walking to the back somewhere to retrieve my dress. "Are you coming tonight?" I asked.

"To the Moody Moon?" she shouted back, "yeah, of course. I'm interested to see what you've done to the place. I only ever stayed there once, but it, er… it sure stays with you!"

"Oh?"

She returned holding up my outfit for tonight and brought out the card machine for me to pay, dropping back down onto her stool and grinning at me with the excitement gossips always have when they share news. "Are you telling me you haven't seen anything *strange* since you got the keys to that place?"

"Strange?"

"You know, things moving, noises you can't explain. I didn't know your grandmother all that well, we were in a book club together for a spell but I think she passed not long after she joined us. Anyway, she said she'd seen some—" The woman looked over my shoulder and stopped talking, she gave a small nod, then turned back to look me in the eye. "You're all paid up, I'll see you tonight. I've got a million things to do and would you look at that? I'm the only one that showed up to work again, no wonder there's..."

As she walked into the back again her voice trailed off and I was left standing alone with only the chatter of seafood enthusiasts for company.

Like I said, my luck ran out while I completing this particular errand. I'd initially thought that parking up outside O'Malley's was the problem, but the *real* issue was that now my car wouldn't start. I wasn't just parked outside O'Malley's, I was stuck there. Oh, and then I had a hot flush. I was sat in the driver's seat of my crappy car and I couldn't turn it on to use the AC and I was sweating through my shirt.

I didn't have time to wait for a tow truck or AAA. Did I even have AAA? I pulled out my phone with a view to calling a taxi, before I could activate the screen the black glass acted like a mirror and I could see the glisten of moisture across my forehead, hair clinging to my skin. Now I needed to add 'take a quick shower' to my to-do list.

The man on the end of the line answered with, "it's going to be a forty minute wait."

"What? You don't even know what I was about to say," I countered.

"All our cars are out and we don't have anyone free for at least forty minutes. I don't know if you're interested but they're doing a 'kids eat free' at Catch of the Day, we've been shuttling tourists there all afternoon."

I couldn't wait here for that long, I'd have to walk. "Never mind," I said, hanging up. The whole reason I'd taken the car out this morning was so that I didn't have to waste time walking around town, and now I was going to have to do that anyway *and* sort out a tow truck. I tried Lena's number, no answer. I tried Michelle, no answer. "Come on!" I urged, trying Lena again.

I got out of the car, grabbed my dress – still in it's protective plastic – and my bag. If I put some pep in my step I could be back at Moody Moon in less than ten minutes and then take the fastest shower anyone has ever had. I had to walk directly passed O'Malley's, the door was propped open and I could hear people inside starting their weekend early.

"Keep going," I heard. It was the same voice I'd heard outside the hotel earlier, a voice that seemed to come out of nowhere. Is this what the woman in the dry cleaners had been talking about? I picked up speed to get away from O'Malley's as quickly as I could and made my way along Bridge Street, hugging the shoreline as it curved around past Shaded Wood and up to the hotel.

CHAPTER 6

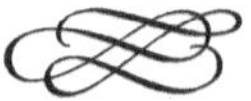

It turned out that you can't just hijack a man for the night from a care home, so Michelle had been escorted by one of the nurses as she wheeled him across from Shaded Wood and up to the hotel. It wasn't Casey, that would have been a total nightmare. I didn't know all of the nurses that worked there, only the ones directly involved in dad's care. The guy standing behind dad's wheelchair wasn't one of his regulars, I really hoped I could avoid having to speak to him so I could avoid the awkward conversation where I had to confess I didn't remember his name.

Given that I'd had to shower twice today to cleanse myself of sweat, the last thing I needed was for a perky chested twenty-something to bounce in here looking like she fell out of a Victoria's Secret window display.

I made a short speech about the legacy of the hotel, posed for photos for Gemma who came back to get a few snaps to accompany the article, and given a guided tour of the pool area, the breakfast nook and a few of the rooms. Finger food was served pool side, small bite-sized snacks to keep everyone happy as they wandered around talking to each other.

I ate a few canapes over a napkin to avoid dropping food on my dress, then wandered back towards reception to dispose of it in the trash can, adding 'buy more trash cans' to a mental checklist. It was then that I noticed the empty bag of potato chips in the trash – Gemma's from earlier. Beneath that was the torn-up invitation to Jack and Casey's engagement party.

Did I tear it up? I thought I'd just put it on the desk with all the other mail. Maybe Lena had done it? I looked back through the glass doors to the pool area and spotted Lena talking animatedly to my sister. There were stood next to my dad who had a huge smile on his face. He was now accompanied by a different nurse, this one I did recognize. It didn't really matter, it wasn't like I planned to go to that thing anyway, and even if I did I didn't need reminding where it was being held.

The front door of the hotel opened and Chris walked through. Had I invited him? Maybe Michelle has seen him when she went over to collect our dad earlier. My brain felt totally scrambled, something I attributed to the stress of organizing tonight.

"Wow, this place looks great!" he said as he came in.

"Thanks, I would say the hard part's over but I think the hard part hasn't started yet!" I replied.

"I didn't know what to bring, so…" he shrugged, handing me a small potted plant. "I went to the gift place just off the bridge and asked for advice, I think a plant is supposed to be for a house warming but I don't know what you are supposed to get for someone opening a business."

"You're the only one that brought something memorable, so you get bonus points for that," I smiled. I felt a wave of hit strike me, but not in the way I'd been experiencing recently. It was just on the back of my neck and my cheeks. It wasn't a hot flash, I was blushing. I felt suddenly aware that this man might be flirting with me and I had no idea what to do about it.

"I would have been here sooner but things were a little dramatic over at the home," he continued.

"Everybody okay?" I asked. I knew from experience that typically when someone works in a healthcare setting describes their day as 'dramatic', they are often referring to multiple medical emergencies.

"Yeah, it's just been one of those days. You probably know the feeling, you were a nurse weren't you?"

"I was… who told you that?" Had Casey been talking about me to Chris? Why did the thought of that make me feel so violated? I was trying to avoid her, I was trying to pretend I'd never even known her at all, but was she talking about me to people?

"Your sister mentioned it," he replied. I'd placed the plant on the reception desk next to one of the bouquets of flowers from earlier – not the one's from Jack, obviously, as they were out in the trash. Chris was idly fiddling with the vase closest to him, nudging it and turning it slightly as if trying to get it into the perfect spot. "Where did you get these from? They're beaut—" he tilted the vase to try and look at the bottom of it to find a label.

He lost control of it and it began to slide out of his grasp, threatening to pour water all over the computer on the reception desk. The *brand new* computer.

"No!" I gasped, throwing my hands forward to catch it. The pot of money that had come with the deeds to this hotel was almost gone, if this computer got damaged it could take weeks before the insurance paid out for a replacement, if they paid out at all.

Everything seemed to stop, as if I was moving through a photograph. I grabbed the vase which appeared to be balanced precariously along the bottom edge at a forty-five degree angle. I wrapped my hands around it, not paying enough attention to the fact that it should have fallen over, it shouldn't have been possible for me to catch it in time.

I looked back at Chris and saw his face locked in shock, he was mid-gasp with his eyes wide and his hands out trying to catch the vase himself. He wasn't moving. I stepped a little closer to him to look at his eyes, he didn't blink.

"Let him go," the familiar voice whispered through the air.

"What?" I replied aloud, turning in place to see if there was anyone else with me.

"Theresa Chase, stop messing with that man," it said.

"But how do I—?" I began, but then whatever had caused Chris to freeze in place *stopped*, and he lurched forward strangely, his hands swiping at the empty space where the vase should have been – only it was now in my arms.

"What the—?" he muttered, a mixture of confusion and embarrassment on his face. He didn't finish asking his question, which was a relief given that I didn't have an answer.

"Thanks again for the plant," I smiled, hoping he wouldn't notice the sweat beads forming on my skin. I could feel it soaking into my bra, the unpleasant sensation of moisture where the cups met in the middle. I cautiously put the vase back on the desk and tried to subtly pull the fabric of my dress away from my back to allow the air to cool me down. Ideally I would be straddling a fan and letting my outfit blow over my head in a less-than-classy homage to Marilyn Monroe.

"Tess, have you—?" Lena began, stopping when she saw Chris in front of me. "Oh… hello. I'm Lena, aren't you a handsome thing."

"Lena," I snapped. "I'm sorry about her, she doesn't get out much."

Chris extended his left hand to shake Lena's, and that's when I spotted the wedding ring. Lena met my eye, but I quickly looked away. I felt embarrassed that I even *entertained* the idea that this man was flirting with me. I wanted a hole to open up in the middle of the ground so that I could fall into it and hide, just ride out the shame in private.

"Tess, I was just going to say that people are starting to get back to their cars so did you want help wrapping this thing up?" Lena asked. "I can stay as late as you need me." She pressed her lips together in a flat line, I knew that look. It was her way of offering silent sympathy, although it felt a little like pity, or that she was cringing on my behalf.

"Do you need an extra pair of hands?" Chris offered.

"No thank you…" Lena said, dragging out the last word as she held a space open for him to provide his name.

"Chris," he added.

"Yes, we can manage by ourselves, *Chris.*" I stifled a laugh, she'd said his name as if she thought he'd provided an alias and that she was onto him.

"Well…" Chris clasped his hands together in front of him, the wrinkles around his eyes deepening as he smiled at me. "Sorry I missed the whole thing tonight, but I have some family coming from out of town soon and it would be great if I could set them up with a stay here. I don't have the space at my house to host them all."

"Let me know the dates and I'll get you all set up," I said. He nodded, then turned to leave.

* * *

LENA HAD BROUGHT a cooler with a box of wine and a few cans of beer. It was my job to provide the blanket and all of the baggage that we would be discussing at length as we stared out at sea. Low tide was at seven o'clock, meaning we could access the island from around five. We'd crossed the land bridge and made our way to one of our favorite spots.

As teens we'd come over here, giant groups of us would cross over at low tide and hang out for ours, sometimes having to sprint back over the bridge with water lapping at our ankles. Over the years the giant group splintered into small groups, then eventually Lena and I were a party of two.

"Have you heard of dating apps?" she said, cracking open a beer and handing it to me.

"Heard of them? Of course I've heard of them. How old do you think I am!?" I laughed.

"Well I hadn't until Molly mentioned it. She said she'd help me set up a profile on one of them, I could ask her to help you as well if you like the sound of it."

"Are you ready for that?" I asked. "From what I hear there are a lot of guys on those things that are only after one thing."

"I know but… well I haven't done *that one thing* in a few years so maybe it's time to get back on the horse, so to speak," she said.

"Lena Whitman!" I laughed.

"Something's got to give, Tess. We were both married for decades and now look at us, two women *of a certain age* that aren't getting any younger, the husbands are gone and we're back up here like we were in high school, talking about boys."

"*You* are talking about boys, I am quite happy to sit here with my drink and forget about men entirely. Jack's having his engagement party tonight, the whole reason we're here is to take my mind off it."

"I don't think it'll last, if you want my opinion," she huffed.

"I don't, but thanks," I replied. "Hey, can I ask you a question without you giving me a concerned look?"

"Depends on the question."

"Do you believe in ghosts?" I asked.

"You still think your grandma is trying to contact you from the other side?" she said, cocking an eyebrow. I wanted to explain about the smoke, the clarity of the voice I'd heard, but her phone started to ring before I had the chance. She pulled it out of her bag and grimaced at the screen before answering, "hello? Well I... I worked last weekend, so... alright, I'll be half an hour," she huffed.

"Hospital?" I guessed.

"They're low on staff and you know how the weekends can get," she said, slowly climbing to her feet. "You coming?"

"I think I'll stay for a bit longer," I replied. I'd seen 'Eat, Pray, Love' enough times to surmise that being alone in a beautiful place can help the post-divorce mind. Maybe that wasn't the right takeaway from the movie.

"Well text me when you get home, okay?"

"Sure," I nodded. She bent to give me a kiss on the cheek and then walked back in the direction of the trail that had brought us up here. It wasn't until she was long gone that I realized she'd left the cooler. I drank the beer she'd handed to me and then lay down on the blanket looking up at the twilight sky. I wasn't sure how long I'd been up here, but night was rolling in and I would have to get going soon before the whole place was too dark to navigate.

I sat up, expecting to look out at the uninterrupted horizon. There was someone standing in front of me. A scream caught in my throat, no sound left my mouth as I stared at the face of the figure. I grabbed hold of my empty beer can as if it could be used as a weapon.

"You cannot kill me twice," she said. *She* being my grandmother. My *dead* grandmother.

"Wh— what is happening?" I gasped. I felt a strange tingling in my hands, like I'd been leaning on them for too long and I'd cut off the blood supply. The sound of the ocean crashing against the island's edges grew louder.

"I thought you might have figured out what you were capable of by yourself, but I see that you stuffed all my old books into a box in your attic," she announced. "Theresa, some of those books are hundreds of years old. You need to treat them with respect!"

I glanced back at the beer can in my hand, scanning the side of it for the alcohol content. Maybe this was some sort of drunken mirage. *Zero percent?* Lena brought alcohol free beer? Not the problem to be focusing on in the moment.

"They were dusty," I said in defense. I'd moved a collection of books from the reception area because they made the place look cluttered. I hadn't even looked at them, I just threw them in a box and got them out of the hotel.

"How else do you expect to learn about witchcraft, young lady? I have had to project myself back into the land of the living because you seem to have missed every clue."

"Witchcraft?" I grimaced.

"Your powers are getting stronger, you froze a man earlier did you not? You need an education before you do some real damage!"

My grandmother stepped forward, or rather *floated* towards me, and her face came into real focus. Her smile was the same, her round cheeks and bright eyes looked exactly as I remembered them. Only she was translucent. She reached out a hand to touch my shoulder and it passed right through me. It was around then that I passed out.

CHAPTER 7

$\mathcal{I}$ woke suddenly, gasping and sitting upright expecting to be still on the blanket on Kettle Island with the beer can in my hand and a ghost stood at my feet. There was no blanket beneath me, just my mattress, and the can in my hand was in fact just a fist full of my bed sheets. I was at home.

I could see a box on the carpet by my wardrobe doors, it was the box of old books from the hotel that I'd stuffed into the attic. It was still sealed with tape, but why was it there? How had it gotten out from the attic? How had *I* gotten home from the island?

The sunlight was flooding the room and I looked back at the nightstand to see the time. It was almost nine o'clock in the morning. When was the last time I ever slept in so late? I shuffled back so I could lean against the pillows, then reached for my phone. I'd never seen so many missed calls before. Michelle had called, so had Lena, so had the guy who had cleaned out the pool a few days ago and so had… *Jack?*

He'd called me late last night, just once.

Had he left a voicemail? If he had, would I even want to listen to it? My phone buzzed as a text message came through from Michelle *'get to the hotel, now.'*

I jumped out of bed, grabbed some clothes and hurried down the stairs. It wasn't until I opened the front door and looked out at my empty driveway that I remembered my car wasn't there. I'd left it on the street on Friday, it had been there for two nights. I knew why I'd avoided going back there yesterday, it was parked right outside O'Malley's and I didn't want to accidentally bump into the happy couple celebrating their engagement.

I stepped back into the house and tried Lena's number. No answer. Michelle ended the call after two rings so I figured she was busy with something, although she had *just* text me to say I needed to get to the hotel. I swapped my sandals for sneakers and decided to try and jog to the Moody Moon. I hadn't done any running in months, so I wasn't going to be breaking any records today, but it would be the fastest way to get across town.

I passed the bakery on Barksdale Drive, turned onto Bridge street and followed the road as it curved, passing the care home until the hotel came into view. I could see the flashing lights outside, a flurry of activity by the entrance to Moody Moon. There were police cars, and an ambulance. I spotted the work van of the pool guy.

"Tess!" Michelle shouted.

"What's going on?" I said. There was a strange flapping noise, and as I got closer I could see that it was the sound of crime scene tape dancing in the wind. "What happened?"

"The pool guy left some tools behind the other day, or so he says. He told us he tried to call but you didn't answer, so he drove over anyway hoping to find you. He said the back gate was open so he figured he could just sneak in and get what he needed, but..." Michelle explained, stopping herself as the squeaky wheel of a gurney pierced the air.

There was someone on the gurney, the shape of a person beneath a white sheet. Another officer stepped towards me, but their voice started to fade into the background as I tracked the gurney on its way to the ambulance.

"Who is that?" I said, ignoring the hum of the male officer.

"Tess, I tried to call," she replied.

"Who is it?" I repeated.

"It's Casey," she said. "The pool guy found her, she was floating face down in the—" she cut herself off. Reluctantly nodding for her colleague to continue with whatever he had been trying to say. The ambulance doors closed and my heart started pounding.

"Do you understand what I'm saying to you? We need you to come in for questioning, Ms. Chase," the officer repeated. The voice came into focus and I turned to see the uniformed man beside me.

"Am I under arrest?" I asked.

* * *

MICHELLE BROUGHT a coffee through from the small kitchen area of the station and handed it to me. It was in a mug that said 'I like big busts and I cannot lie' with a cartoonish sketch of two officers hand-cuffing a man in a suit beside a huge pile of cash.

"We love a novelty mug around here," she said, sitting next to me on a faded green sofa in the staff room of the Kettle Harbor police department. "How are you feeling?"

"Confused," I replied, taking a sip of the brown sludge and recoiling slightly.

"I know, it was Steve's turn to restock the drinks cupboard and he got the worst instant coffee on planet earth. We have a proper machine over there, I explicitly told him we needed *beans* and yet—" she stopped herself mid-rant and put a reassuring hand on my leg. "Look, I just asked that you get a minute to compose yourself before the questioning starts, that's why we're back here."

"What happened to Casey?" I asked. "How did she end up in the hotel pool? When did all this happen?"

"We don't have all the facts yet, we're working on it. Look, I know how much this is all messing with you, what with Gran showing up and—"

"Hold on, you've seen Gran?"

"Yeah… she told me not to say anything, but listen—" Michelle leaned closer as if she were about to tell me a secret, but before she had the chance to, the door to the staff room opened and the male officer from earlier stepped through.

"Is now a good time?" he asked.

"That depends, is Charlotte here yet, Steve?" Michelle asked. Steve gulped nervously, then nodded. "Then yes, now *is* a good time. Charlotte will look after you, Tess. I'm going to head out to get some proper beans for the coffee machine because *somebody* messed up at the store."

"But—" I managed. Michelle had been about to tell me something, I didn't want this conversation to be over, I didn't want to have to go into an interrogation room without her.

"You'll be fine, just do whatever Charlotte says," she nodded. My older sister stood up and walked out of the room.

"Ms. Chase, this way," Steve said. I got to my feet and, on unsteady legs, carried the novelty mug full of coffee flavored slime out of the staff room and along the corridor. We turned a corner and came face-to-face with a stern looking woman in a power suit who was impatiently tapping her right heeled shoe against the floor tiles.

"I need to speak to my client alone, so beat it, Steve," she spoke.

"Y— yes, ma'am," he nodded. It was more than a nod though, he seemed to bend at the waist as if he was bowing to royalty.

"He's not the brightest bulb in the chandelier," she smiled. "Charlotte Brooks, nice to meet you again."

"Again?"

"Oh, you don't remember? Let's sit down and we can talk about what's happening, I'm under the impression you're able to hear it all now," she explained, pushing open the door to the interrogation room and gesturing for me to step inside.

There was one of those large mirror things that I'd seen on TV, the one that usually separated the criminals from the cops that were secretly watching the interview. I caught sight of my reflection in it, ghostly pale and with my hair slightly frizzed. Having ash blonde hair meant that the greys didn't show all that much, not that it stopped me from regularly dying them out however.

I pulled out the plastic chair and lowered myself onto it, watching as Charlotte pulled out a number of documents from a briefcase that I hadn't noticed until we'd got into the room. "Do I need you here because the cops think I killed Casey?" I asked.

"I don't know if we've gotten to the point of throwing accusations around just yet, they have a dead body and a motive so it's important we get ahead of this thing before you *do* find yourself in trouble," she explained.

"I've never needed a lawyer before…" I mumbled. "I mean, I had a divorce lawyer but—"

"Your grandmother's estate, I was the one she assigned to make sure everything was handled properly after her death. At that time you weren't ready to hear the entirety of your inheritance, but I have been informed that you now qualify."

"Qualify? What are you talking about?" I said, finding myself growing irritated. I lay my forearms on the table and leaned forward, "who called you? Was it my sister?"

"I am the family lawyer, no one needed to call me. I was summoned here for two reasons, one being the unfortunate end of that young woman's life, and the other being that you are coming into your magic," she continued, matter-of-factly. She shuffled a stack of papers and slid them across the table towards me. "I'll need you to sign these, just a box-ticking exercise really but it's important to have all the paperwork in place just in case."

I read the words across the top of the first page, 'The Chase Family Legacy'. *This document represents an agreement between [CLIENT] and [AGENCY]. The [CLIENT] hereby accepts the gift of the CHASE FAMILY LEGACY, as set out in THE CHASE COLLECTION. In signing is document, [CLIENT] agrees to—*

"What on earth is this?" I said, looking up at Charlotte who had produced an emery board and was filing her left thumbnail. "What is this talking about?"

"You're a witch, it seems pretty obvious," she replied, not looking away from her nails as she spoke. From the corner of her eye she must have seen my mouth hanging open, so decided to give me her full attention. "Your grandmother has been trying to reach you, I suppose she planned to explain all this to you herself. At some point you had an ancestor that decided it would be—" she lifted up her hands to make air quotes, "—'more fun' if you gained access to your powers during 'the change'. The idea caught on and now the whole harbor operates that way."

"Excuse me?" I said, looking horrified.

"Look, I didn't come up with it, I'm just passing along the information. One part of your life is now in the rearview mirror, maybe you think all the excitement you'll ever have is behind you. That's where *this* comes in," she said, tapping at the paperwork. "The next part of your life will be more exciting than the last part, so long as we keep you out of jail obviously."

"Jail? I thought you said they weren't accusing me of anything!" I gasped. "Is this supposed to be a joke? Did Michelle put you up to this to cheer me up? I'm not *that* cut up about my ex getting re-married. She didn't need to set up some weirdly elaborate prank to make me think I was about to jet off to Hogwarts or something. I want to speak to my sister." I huffed and leaned back in the chair, eyeing the door as if waiting for someone to burst through it and tell me there'd been a mistake and nobody was dead.

"Have you seen your grandmother's ghost? Yes or no."

"Well I… I'd thought that I… I've been under a lot of pressure lately and…"

"I'll take that as a yes," she interrupted. "I also had a report that you used your magic on Friday to freeze time, is that correct?"

"No, what happened was—"

"Your sister has powers too, so did your grandmother, so did your mom. You can't learn about this world until you have powers of your own, Ms. Chase. It's not my job to help you navigate the world of magic, just making sure that you don't accidentally use your powers in front of a human and get yourself in trouble. I've been made aware that you have located the books, so you can work through those at your leisure," she said.

"The books from my attic?"

"I don't know where you were keeping them," she shrugged.

"Could you—?" She handed me a pen and nudged the paperwork closer to me. How could she have known about the books? About gran's ghost? About the incident with Chris? In a daze, I began to sign my name in every blank space. My pen had barely left the final page before Charlotte reached her hand to grab them.

She took the stack of papers and threw them over her shoulder, but instead of falling to the ground in a mess… they disappeared.

"Now that we've taken care of that, I need to ask you about the deceased," she began.

I could feel the beginnings of a migraine coming on, an ache right between my eyebrows that was spreading slowly. I put my elbows on the table and leaned on my hands, using my fingers to massage at my forehead hoping that it might ease the tension. I took a deep breath and closed my eyes for a second. Two days ago my biggest problem was trying to find a parking space in town, how could everything have changed so quickly.

CHAPTER 8

"ow well did I know her? Not well enough, clearly," I sighed. "I mean, I worked with her for a short time, then…"

"Yes?" Charlotte prodded.

"Well then I caught her and my husband *in flagrante delicto* in our bed, so—"

"You saw them?"

"Yeah, and do you know what Jack had the nerve to say to me? I walk in and catch the two of them naked as the day they were born and he says *'you weren't supposed to be back for another hour'*. Can you believe that? As if the main issue with the whole mess was that I'd gotten off a shift early, that it all would have been totally fine if I'd have just been out of the house as long as I initially planned to be," I huffed, the anger of that moment hitting was still as potent now as it had been all those months ago. *Time heals all wounds?* If that were true then how would grudges exist, huh?

Charlotte raised an eyebrow at me and clasped her hands together on the table, "have you seen her since then?"

"She took a job at the care home where my dad lives, but I try to only visit when she isn't working," I replied.

"Do you have an alibi?"

"For when? Last night? When did she...?" I began. Then I realized I didn't have an alibi, I had been out on Kettle Island and then blacked out, only to wake up in my bed. Was I supposed to say that to the police? That I had a lapse in memory *conveniently* covering the window of time when Casey would have died, but that I was *pretty* sure I hadn't murdered anyone. I shook my head slowly.

A knock on the door preceded Steve stepping back into the room.

"Why knock if you're just going to come in anyway?" Charlotte asked.

"Aren't you ready?" he asked, looking at his wristwatch as if he couldn't comprehend that a conversation could possibly last this long. Maybe he didn't realize that this lawyer had begun by dropping a bombshell about witchcraft on me and that I had been expected to put a pin in that piece of information and put it to one side to instead defend myself in a potential murder investigation.

Charlotte stood up, collected her things, and walked around the table to sit beside me. She leaned in as she sat down again, "say as little as possible."

Steve sat down and was joined by another officer I hadn't met before, the two men faced us across the table. "Ms. Chase, where were you between the hours of nine o'clock last night and nine o'clock this morning?" he began.

"Bed," I said. How's that for 'as little as possible'?

"Can anyone vouch for that?"

"No."

"Are you aware of anyone who might have had access to the gate at the back of Moody Moon Motel?" he continued.

"It's a hotel," I corrected. "I know 'motel' works better alliteratively, but—" Charlotte gave me a light kick under the table. "No."

"When was the last time you saw Casey Quinn?"

"Friday, at Shaded Wood," I answered. The door opened, this time without a knock. It was Michelle.

"Steve, how is she still here? I thought you only had a few questions, I've been to the store and back in the time it's taken you to—"

she stepped into the room and picked up his notepad, "establish that she has no alibi? That took you forty minutes?"

"No, but—" he stuttered defensively.

"Look, Tess, you're a person of interest at this time but until we have more specific questions you may as well get out of here," Michelle explained.

"Person of interest? Wait, you think I killed her?"

"No, not a *suspect*," she clarified.

"Not yet," Steve mumbled.

"I'm tempted to roll up a newspaper and swat you on the nose," Michelle snapped. "Tess, go home. I'll be round in a few hours, okay? And Steve, come with me. I'm going to show you how that coffee machine works because if you get instant again I will discharge my weapon in your general direction, got it?"

Steve and the other officer scuttled out as Michelle held the door open for them. I stood up and walked over to the door, then turned back to see if Charlotte was actually done with me yet. No doubt I'd need her contact information and she would need to tell me what was supposed to happen next, not to mention elaborate on the whole 'you're a witch' thing. But she was gone. The room had one door and she hadn't walked through it, yet the room was now empty.

"What happened?" I asked, looking to Michelle for answers.

"Get home, Tess. I'll explain it all later."

* * *

MICHELLE HAD OFFERED ME A RIDE, but I'd declined. I was still wearing my sneakers from earlier, so was more than capable of walking home by myself. I stepped out of the police station and inhaled the briny air of Kettle Harbor, unsure of how everything about my hometown could feel the same and simultaneously like an alien place.

My legs felt heavy as I headed for Bridge Street, I wanted to follow the coast as I journey home and let the sight of the water lapping at the shore puncture the mounting panic within me. There was a somber atmosphere at the beach, even the tourists seemed to sense that something was going on. By now it was probably common knowledge that there'd been a death, and judging by the stares in my direction it would appear people knew *where* Casey was found.

The ache from my short run earlier made it hard to pick up much speed, my body didn't recover from exercise in the way it had when I was in my twenties, but I couldn't stand the accusatory glances and so hurried home while keeping my head down. I passed the bakery, briefly considered stopping in for twenty dollars' worth of sugary comfort food, but ultimately decided to carry on home. I was sure I had cookie dough in the house anyway.

The figure sitting on my front porch was the *last* person I'd expected to see, especially as I wasn't even aware he knew where I lived.

Jack looked up when he heard my footsteps approaching, he'd been hunched over with his head in his hands and his eyes were bloodshot. I'd loved that man most of my adult life, and in one moment – the moment where I'd caught him cheating – he had become forever altered in my mind.

There was no way to look at his face, his familiar features and kind eyes, without instantly remembering how much he'd hurt me. I didn't say anything as I got closer, I just pulled out my keys and walked to the door.

"Tess," he said, climbing up onto his feet. I put my key in the lock and turned it, pushed the door open, then looked back. He was a sorry sight. It looked like he'd shed a few pounds, I hated that for some reason. I noticed then that he had a scratch on his neck, in fact he had a couple of them. I noticed his right hand, the knuckles bloodied.

"I suppose you want a coffee," I smiled. I wasn't sure what had happened to him, but given that his fiancé had just been found face down in my hotel pool it didn't seem like the time to add a hostile conversation to his list of concerns.

This had been one of the problems when we'd been married, I'd put his needs before my own. Even now, when I would have every right to tell him to take his ass back home and cry on someone else's shoulder, I was welcoming him into my house and filling up the kettle.

After our split I'd slept on Michelle's couch for a week. Lena had taken me in for almost a month, but after a while you just need your own space to wallow in self-pity. I'd half-considered staying at the hotel, but I'd been creeped out by the place when I'd first taken ownership of it and it was in dire need of repairs and renovations. I rented the nicest place I could afford – which was not as nice as the house I'd shared with Jack – and then started to get to work on fixing up Moody Moon.

I couldn't stand the thought of seeing Jack and Casey together, so much so that I'd walked away from my career just to give myself an easy way to avoid them. It was for my sanity, I wasn't sure that I could resist the urge to strangle that idiot with his own tie if I saw him again. He was lucky he wasn't wearing one now, actually.

He took himself into the living room and a few minutes later I brought in a coffee – milk and two sugars –without the need to ask him how he took it. As much as I wish I could throw away that useless information, apparently I'd remembered it.

"Thanks," he said, taking the mug from my hand. I got a better look at his right hand as he reached out to grab his drink, it was as if he'd punched something. "What have they told you?"

"What has *who* told me?"

"The police, they took you to the station didn't they? I thought you might have heard something about what happened, about how..." He took a deep, unsteady breath and then sipped at his coffee as if to calm himself. "They didn't tell me much, they just came to tell me that she was... I heard where she was found and I just..."

"They just wanted to know how someone could have got in to the pool area, that's pretty much all they asked me."

"And?" he pressed.

"Well, I don't know. I suppose there's a chance I didn't lock the gate on Friday night, but I usually check," I shrugged.

"Don't you have cameras? Some sort of security?" he pressed, his tone a little more sharp now, almost as if he was building up to an accusation.

"They get fitted this week, I didn't need it sorting ahead of the party so—"

"Convenient," he huffed. "Very convenient. You know, when I heard you'd been put into the back of a police car I wasn't even that surprised. The fact that they let you out again so soon? Seems as though being related to the chief of police lets you get away with murder in this town, literally."

"Well, it was nice seeing you again Jack but it's time for you to get the hell out of my house now," I said, standing. I snatched the coffee out of his hands and put it down on an end table behind me.

"So you're saying you're not a suspect?"

"Why would I want her dead? What would I gain from that?" I yelled.

"Revenge, for one thing. We were gonna be so happy, Tess. You couldn't stand it, you couldn't stand the idea that I had moved on," he barked, now on his feet and running his hands through his greying hair. "Everyone's gonna think it was you, everyone."

"You have five seconds to leave or I'm going to start throwing things, one, two three..." I reached for a lamp.

"Fine, I'll go." He looked at me for a second, pressing his lips together in the way he used to do when he was about to say something, but was trying to select the right words. He opened his mouth, thought better of it, then left.

I muttered to myself as I carried his coffee back to the kitchen and tipped it down the sink, "if I have a motive to kill anyone, it's you. You big, stupid man. How is he a doctor? What an idiot?! I can't believe that I—" The sudden appearance of my grandmother's ghost stopped me in my tracks, her body only visible from the waist up as she was stood *in* my cleaning cupboard, erupting through the counter with a disappointed look on her face.

I clutched my chest, the mug slamming against my collar bone and causing me to grimace in pain. To my surprise, and perhaps hers, I didn't scream or pass out. I laughed.

"What is so funny?" she asked.

"It's just so ridiculous that it feels like laughing is the only appropriate way to react," I replied, "have you come to tell me about a buried treasure that only you know the location of? Or maybe you were murdered and you want me to avenge your death?"

"I am not sure that I approve of your tone. Firstly, I am not a pirate, and secondly, I died in my sleep. Not much to avenge there, unfortunately. I understand that Charlotte has filled you in on some of the details," she said, moving away from the counter and into the middle of the kitchen.

If it had been any other ghost I think I would have been terrified, but this wasn't a stranger – it was my grandma. The woman that helped raise Michelle and I after my mom took off, and treated my dad like her son even though he wasn't. She kept the family together even when the tragedy tried to pull it apart and I think that's what made my divorce feel all the harder, she wasn't there to hold my hand through it.

She was affectionate in her own way, not one for verbalizing her love for us so much but she went out of her way to make elaborate birthday cakes and costumes for parties, taught us the name of every plant in her back yard and kept us nourished with books every summer, when it came to shopping at the book store she never said no to anything we picked up.

"That I'm a witch? Yeah, it came up," I nodded.

"I should have told you myself, but you made it difficult for me to appear to you since my death. You closed your mind off to it somehow, I was not aware that it was something you could do. I was plagued by ghosts all my life and yet you managed to block them out before you even gained access to your powers!"

I pinched my fingers against the bridge of my nose and closed my eyes, a brief reality check to see if she would still be there when I opened them. She was. "Okay, so I'm a witch and so's Mich. What am I supposed to do with that information? The only thing that would help me right now would be if I could magic up an alibi for last night because currently it looks like I'm suspect numero uno for a murder, Gran."

"You used your magic to bring yourself home from the island. It is not something the police are likely to appreciate hearing, well there is actually a spell in place to make sure that our secrets are not spilled by loose lipped ladies! There is a box of books upstairs that you can start with, Michelle can help you when she arrives," she explained. "A *potential* was murdered, Theresa. This affects all of us, you know."

"A potential?"

"Casey would have been a witch if she had made it to the right age, which means she was what we call a potential. It could mean that there is someone targeting our kind… *your* kind to me specific. I am not entirely sure if I am still a witch if I am a ghost, I have yet to try out my powers since my death. Anyway, get reading!"

CHAPTER 9

I sat on my bedroom carpet floor with the cardboard box open and the contents spilled out. There had to be at least fifteen books inside, each one had cracks in the spine and dog-eared pages. It was obvious they'd been read over and over, some of the covers had faded, the titles now barely readable.

I glanced over at my nightstand and the enormous *to be read* pile of books next to my lamp. I'd bought a few self help books, a 'clinicians guide to the menopause' which I'd yet to open because it looked depressing, a couple of romance novels and a well-loved copy of the first Harry Potter book.

The rest of the Hogwarts adventures were kept on a shelf downstairs, but the first one stayed next to my bed. I'd read it to Lena's kids, to my nieces, and I'd hoped to read it to my own children but life didn't go that way for Jack and I. Still, I held onto them. Sometimes I would take myself upstairs for an early night and read all of *Sorcerer's Stone* in one sitting, I'd even bought a copy of the English version *Philosopher's Stone* and compared them page by page to see if there were any differences.

Maybe the fact that I had time to do that should have been a red flag that my marriage was on the rocks, because Jack and I barely ever saw each other towards the end.

Michelle let herself in and called my name. "I'm up here!" I yelled back. The thud of her shoes on my stairs – my *carpeted* stairs that were now going to need vacuuming because I knew she'd have left a trail of dirt – preceded her stomping into my room.

"How's it going?" she asked, dropping onto the floor beside me and picking up a book from the pile that had an emerald green cover and a title printed in gold ink.

"Oh, well the ghost of our dead grandma showed up in the kitchen and told me to come and read all the books about witchcraft that I've had in the attic for the past six months. She mentioned that you were a witch, and that mom was too. Oh, and that maybe Casey was murdered because she was a 'potential', and I think I've got a varicose vein here," I said, catching sight of my bare left calf.

"You should probably see a doctor," she replied, smiling at me as she intentionally avoided commenting on everything else I said. I jabbed her in the ribs with the book I was holding. "I guess you probably have some questions, but I would like it on record that I was specifically told my Gran not to mention any of this to you until it was time."

"So her ghost came to you and you kept it from me?"

"Well I turned forty when Gran was still alive, do you remember my fortieth birthday party had Gran had *way* too much to drink and started dancing on the table at that restaurant?"

"Vividly," I laughed.

"Yeah, well I'd not managed to book the next day off at work so I wasn't drinking. I offered to drive her home and then she started spewing all this crazy in the car, talking about magic and mom and how it was 'my time' to find out. I thought it was the tequila talking, but then when we got back to her place she..." Michelle paused, smiling at a memory, "she showed me. I watched her click her fingers and her entire outfit changed.

"I thought maybe she had some of those tear-away pants like strippers do, you know? I thought she was just trying to trick me or something. Then she did it again, then she snapped her fingers and changed *my* clothes. She then fell onto her bed fast asleep, so I went back to the party and tried to carry on with the night but it was hard to forget about it all. She showed up at the station the next day when my shift was over and we went for a walk. That's when she told me everything."

"So you can do magic?" I asked, my brows crinkled into a skeptical frown. Despite having seen a ghost in the past hour, I was still hesitant to believe any of it.

Michelle clicked her fingers and the pile of books on my nightstand floated up into the air, travelled towards me, and landed at my feet. She eyed the copy of Harry Potter and laughed. "It's not quite like any of that, you are unlikely to find yourself getting into a war with a group of dark wizards or whatever, but it's, well— things are interesting now, that's for sure."

I snapped my fingers and nothing happened, then I clicked again.

"Are you auditioning for West Side Story?" Michelle teased. "Look, it happens slowly at first. Acknowledging that any of this is real is step one, the actual magic comes later. You're of age, it won't be long."

I looked at my older sister and tried to assess her expression. As kids when she would try to prank me she would normally start laughing, I could get her to crack with prolonged eye contact. I waited for her to break, to punch me in the shoulder and tell me that I just need to adjust my meds because I sounded crazy. She didn't crack. She reached a hand out and cupped my face with it.

"Is this real?" I asked. She nodded. "Does dad know? I mean, Gran said mom was a witch too, so—"

"Dad knows. He knew that it would probably happen to us too, but he's not been all that talkative lately so, you know," she shrugged. "I don't think he would have been allowed to tell us anyway."

"And Casey?"

"Well, here's the thing about Casey..." Michelle shuffled back so that she could lean against the wall. "She won't have known she was a potential, only other witches know."

"So *you* knew this whole time?" I said.

"I did, but it never really mattered because up until recently you were just a potential too. Gran has always had a thing about hunters, that someone would roll into town and start killing off witches. Do you remember how mom was always scared of the water because she was convinced a shark was going to get her? In the history of Kettle Harbor, how many people have died by shark attack? Zero. She was paranoid about sharks, Gran was paranoid about hunters."

"You don't think that's why Casey was killed?"

"No," she replied. "From what Gran told me, hunters use weapons. There were marks found on her neck, the coroner said her hyoid bone was fractured."

"She was strangled?"

"Yes. My guess would be that she was put in the pool to obscure the true cause of death, maybe the killer was hoping that everyone would just think she drowned. It's an odd choice in terms of a cover up considering that we have the ocean right there, why *your* pool?"

"Jack was here earlier, he thinks I did it," I said.

"Well that's because he's a stupid, stupid man with stupid, stupid friends," she huffed. "I found out a few weeks back that Steve and Jack play golf together. Those two deserve each other, drinking crappy coffee in their golf cart as they talk about things they have no right to be talking about."

"You've lost me."

"I don't think you killed Casey, but if you were the type of person that likes looking at the evidence and who that points to… well then it would look like you had done this, Tess. Steve doesn't know about magic because he's a big dumb-dumb, but I know you were out on that island last night, I know Gran was with you. I'm willing to have her as your alibi, but *legally* speaking you don't actually have anyone that can say where you were last night," she explained.

"So you think Steve told Jack that I did it?" I asked.

"There was a press thing, we asked for anyone who had information to call in. Your name came up," she said. The look of horror on my face prompted her to continue, "it's hardly a secret that your marriage ended because of her, you've been intentionally trying to avoid her at Shaded Wood, making a big ordeal of calling every week to see when she's on shift. *I know you were trying to make sure you didn't see her, but it also is the kind of thing a stalker would do."

"People have really called in to accuse me?"

"You got an invite to the engagement party, Tess. You were on their guest list, Jack gave us a copy," she said.

"Yeah, but I didn't go."

"No, but you knew when it was and where she would be," she continued. "Look, I'm just saying that a lot of fingers are pointed in your direction right now, that's all."

"And *I'm* saying that we need to find out who actually killed her because I don't like the idea that half of Kettle Harbor thinks I murdered a woman, Michelle. Jack thinks I did it *and* that I'll get away with it because I'm your sister. You know what he's like, he'll have spread that theory around town three times over by now," I exclaimed.

"It doesn't mean people will listen. You've got a lot on your plate what with the hotel, the ex-husband accusing you of murder thing, and then magic? I mean, *phew*, I'm glad I'm not you."

"It's always so nice when you drop round, nothing like the reassurance only a sister can provide when life gets tough," I said, sarcastically.

"It's going to get to a point where I might have to step away from this case, Tess. It's going to look like a massive conflict of interest if I ignore the fact that the evidence is pointing at you, I can't have the people of this town start to doubt my professionalism because that becomes a whole other mess. Look, I can nudge you in the right direction but I can't really be involved. Steve's gonna be put on this, and he can barely tie his own shoelaces."

"So I have to clear my own name, somehow. Is that what you're saying?" I asked.

"Steve is going to follow the path of least resistance, you look like the obvious choice. He won't put in the leg work. Casey was at her engagement party and then somehow she's found dead across town in your swimming pool. What did her night look like? Did she leave the party early? Who was with her? Did she get into an argument with anyone? Did she have enemies?" she said.

"So now I'm some sort of low-key witch detective?"

"Well you're not really a witch yet, and to be a detective you'd need a license… but sure!"

I pinched the bridge of my nose and tried to organize my next move in my head. "But you *are* a witch, so can you show me something I can use?"

"I don't know how strong your powers are yet. Have you made anything strange happen?" she asked.

"I got here from Kettle Island somehow… I froze dad's physiotherapist by accident on Friday night… that's about it I think."

"You froze him? That's impressive! I think the first thing I managed to do with my powers was refill a glass of water, so I guess you're leaps and bounds ahead of me. I'll make a few calls and see if I can get the gang together tonight to welcome you properly, they will be better for teaching than I will. Now that you're coming into your powers I'm no longer the newest recruit!"

"What about Lena? Does she have powers?" I asked.

"Yeah, but she got them a year before I did, so she's been with them longer than me. They come around your fortieth birthday, I think Lena got them at thirty-nine so they treated her like a child-prodigy!" she laughed.

"Is it going to be one of those things where there's a bunch of middle-aged women skipping in a circle with no clothes on? I've not been beach ready for about fifteen years, I would have appreciated a heads up."

"You can take your clothes off if you want to, but no one else will be doing that so you're gonna look pretty weird," she smiled.

I glanced over at the bed, I'd left it unmade when I'd raced out of the house this morning. I eyed the creases in the sheets, the duvet folded back and the crooked pillow. A slight warmth in my fingers caused me to look down at my hands, it felt like I'd dipped them into bath water, the temperature slowly rising.

"Tess," Michelle said, nudging me and jerking her chin towards the bed. I looked back and the duvet lifted into the air an inch or two, smoothed itself out, then landed perfectly onto of the mattress. The pillow straightened and the heat in my fingers disappeared.

"Did I—?"

"Of course you're good at all this stuff straight away, you can't let me have anything, can you?" she joked. My heart was racing. It was hardly the same as zooming through the sky on a broomstick or conjuring up a demon, or whatever else witches were supposed to do, but it was *something*. A nervous laugh escaped my mouth and I stared at my hands in amazement.

I just had the small matter of keeping myself out of jail to deal with, and *then* I could let myself enjoy this new chapter of my life.

CHAPTER 10

My car had been towed. I stood on the sidewalk a hundred yards down the street from O'Malley's and stared at the empty parking spot where my car should have been. How much was the fine going to be? Probably more than the car was worth at this point. I should just let them keep it, save my money and buy something better.

Bicycles don't break like that, they're reliable and cheap to run. Wait, do you have to wear those skin tight shorts and shirts that you always see on cyclists? *Urgh*. Pass.

I walked up to the entrance of the bar, the door was open and I could hear the voices of a few customers enjoying an afternoon drink. Did this place serve food now? I couldn't remember when I'd last eaten. I steeled myself for the memories that would no doubt come flooding back as soon as I stepped into the place. I'd had my engagement party here, we'd celebrated friends birthday's here as a couple, toasted the completion of Jack's residency in here.

I stepped in, my eyes adjusting to the dim light that trickled through the stained glass windows. There were whispers when people caught sight of me, I was sure I heard someone say the word *'jealous'* as I walked towards the men polishing glasses by the cash register.

These people thought I'd killed Casey, and they weren't being all that subtle about it.

"Tess, how are ya?" Finn asked, greeting me with a smile I was relieved to see. He'd worked in this place as long as I'd been legally able to drink in it. Somehow he'd worked his way up from bartender to manager, everyone else would get tired of dealing with the weekend rush of folks drinking to excess, but Finn had shown his mettle with crowd control.

"I've been better, how about you?"

"Oh, you know," he shrugged. "I've got the sports crowd coming in at three and that's always a lively group. I had to put bulletproof glass in front of the TV the last time we showed a hockey game because a few folks get a little spirited when their team loses and throw drinks at the screen."

"Charming," I said, hopping up onto a bar stool and surveying the room. Each person that was looking my way turned their heads once I caught their eye.

"Pay no mind, Tess. The rumor mill will churn out something new by the morning," he smiled. "Drink?"

"Thanks, but I can't stay long. I was just hoping to ask you a few questions about last night, actually."

He pressed his lips into a hard line and put the glass he was polishing down. "I guess I should have figured that's why you came round. I haven't seen you in here for months..."

"This place has a lot of memories," I replied.

"Not all bad though," he added. No, they weren't *all* bad. Maybe bad wasn't even the right word, probably 'painful' was better. It's strange how recent events can taint memories from years ago, as if I wouldn't have enjoyed any of the moments I'd spent in here if I'd known one day I'd be divorced and living in a little house by myself.

"Were you here last night?" I asked.

"I sure was. I make a point to be here when we have events booked, even ones I'm not happy about."

"Oh?"

"Well, I heard about... I know that..." Finn leaned his palms against the bar and looked down for a moment, "I think you didn't get treated well in all this mess and I thought it was bold to be getting engaged so soon after—" He cut himself off and gestured at me with his right hand, "I didn't think it was right, that's all. He'd had too many, too fast if you ask me. I stopped serving him at some point because I thought it was getting out of hand. You know how he used to make speeches after a few beers? Some things never change. He shouldn't have been engaged again so soon."

"I appreciate it, but you don't need to worry about me," I smiled. "I'm just trying to figure out what happened last night so that I can get myself out of hot water."

"So I *do* need to worry," he laughed. "Are you sure I can't get you a drink?"

"I'll take a lemonade," I said, wondering if he was suggesting something harder, as if I'd need liquor to get me through what he was about to say.

Finn set about filling a tall glass with ice, "it was going well enough, there were maybe twenty people in here, maybe twenty-five. We had music, there were decorations up, a cake. At one point I heard raised voices, I guess I was out the back getting more beers for the front fridges, I peered out the back door and..."

He set the glass of lemonade down on the bar and nudged it closer to me, the only sound now was the coverage of some football game coming out of the TV and a few conversations from the other side of the room.

"Finn?"

"I saw the girl, she was facing towards the back door. The other person had their back to me so I couldn't see who it was, but there were getting into it a little bit. I don't know what they were talking about but she looked upset, we have a light out the back and it was making her tears shine on her face," he explained.

"What time was that?" I asked.

"Around ten thirty, maybe? I can't be all that sure to be honest with you. The barmaid that was on last night yelled for me to come back in, she needed help with something. I think that was the last time I saw Casey, out in the back alley."

"She didn't come back into the party?"

"I don't think so. I think most of it wrapped up just after eleven, then we had a few hangers on that stayed past midnight," he explained.

"Any chance you've had cameras put back there?"

"I wish. You know what's it's like, the only folk that go out there are smokers trying to get shelter from the wind so they can light their cigarettes. The sidewalk out front is gets the air right off the water, back there it's easier. It's just a service alley, it's delivery trucks and smokers, that's it."

"Do you know if it was a man or a woman out there with Casey?"

"It was a man's voice, he never turned around though," Finn replied, his eyes creasing at the corners as he gave me a sympathetic smile. "For what it's worth, I don't think you killed her, Tess."

"Jeez, thanks," I laughed. A memory leapt back into the front of my mind, the bruises on Casey's temple and wrist. Her friend at Shaded Wood had been comforting her, maybe she'd told this guy what had happened to cause those marks in the first place. Maybe he knew something.

My mouth hung open as I contemplated the fact that often when women are killed it is at their partner's hands.

Jack was an ungrateful, cheating piece of crap that would probably have starved to death when he in his twenties if I hadn't been there to cook all his meals. He outright refused to learn how to operate the washing machine and I was quite sure he never cleaned the bathroom *once* in all the years of our marriage. Who do you suppose was the one that made the bathroom so disgusting? Funny how that worked out, eh?

Just because a guy pees all over the place and leaves *me* to clean up after him, doesn't mean he's capable of murdering someone. Right? Could he have caused those bruises though? He had bloody knuckles and a scratch on his neck, who had he been fighting with? I thought I'd known him, and then he'd turned out to be someone I didn't even recognize. Maybe this was just something else about him that he'd been hiding well.

"Are you alright? You look like you've left your body," Finn said. I'd been staring forward, unblinking, for probably a minute or two.

"Yeah, sorry. Just a lot to take in," I replied. "Thanks for your help, I really appreciate it."

"Any time. I believe I owe you a drink anyway, a little congratulations to the newest business owner in town."

"Business owner? Oh, me! I wouldn't break out the champagne just yet, I'll be lucky to get a single customer staying at the hotel with this hanging over me." One of the many reasons I needed to find out who'd really killed Casey – not that my earning potential was a priority in all this mess. It was obviously more important to imprison the murdered that was running around Kettle Harbor in case they struck again.

"I'll keep a bottle on ice for you, just in case," he said.

I thanked him again and headed back to the sidewalk. I took myself over to Bridge Street, then climbed over the small wall that separated the beach from the rest of town. I stood on the wall for a moment before lowering myself down so I could sit on it. I faced out towards the island; the tide was high and the water consumed almost all of the sand.

"Room for one more?" Before I had a chance to look to my right, Scott was already clambering to sit beside me. I was grateful for the friendly face.

"What are you doing on land?" I asked.

"I'm not out on the water *all* the time, besides the fabric people had a cancellation so they asked if they could move us up on their schedule by a few days. I was dead against it but obviously Lisa was telling me it was happening, rather than asking for my permission," he explained. "What with the swell last night I figured I'd just wait until everything settled."

"Any chance you didn't hear about—?"

"I heard," he said, cutting me off as if sparing me the task of having to say it out loud. "I can't even imagine what the last few days have been like. I barely got to speak to you at your party on Friday, this whole thing is such a mess."

"Yeah," I agreed. For a few moments we sat in the sound of the water. "You know, Jack thinks I killed her. It looks as though he's launched a one-man crusade to spread the word around town. I feel as if everyone's eyes have been on me since I woke up this morning."

"He should be the one getting questioned, if you ask me," Scott huffed. I turned to see his nostrils flare and his jaw harden.

"What do you mean?"

"Lisa moved onto your old street, she's maybe two houses over from your— from Jack's house," he began. My hands rested on the wall either side of my hips and I felt them ball into fists like a reflex at the notion that the house I'd helped build for all those years was now just known to the world as 'Jack's house'. "She heard arguing coming from there all the time, they weren't the happy couple they were pretending to be."

"But they just got engaged," I said. "Why would you get engaged if you were both making each other miserable."

"Beats me," he shrugged. "You know, Lisa said she called the cops once because the yelling was so loud. I don't know why they aren't grilling Jack about all this, that would be my guess as to why he's trying to put you in the spotlight because he's trying to cover himself."

"She called the cops?"

"Yeah, she said a patrol car showed up and went inside the house to speak to them. I don't know if Michelle is allowed to tell you stuff like that about work, I thought it was only doctors that have to do the whole confidentiality thing."

"I don't know... I guess I've never asked." I used my hands to turn me in place so that I could dangle my legs down on the sidewalk-side of the wall, before hopping down. I looked along Bridge Street in the general direction of Shaded Wood. I wanted to speak to the nurse that had been comforting Casey last week when I'd spotted those bruises, I needed to know if Michelle knew about this situation at 'Jack's house'.

I was supposed to see Michelle later, she was arranging a meeting of other witches in town and thankfully I had enough other stuff going on today that I couldn't dwell on the idea. Witches in Kettle Harbor, a town famed for having more seafood restaurants per square mile than any other coastal town in the continental US, who would have believed it?

I looked at Scott for a moment and wondered if he knew about the big secret, I'd only been clued in a few hours ago, but maybe he had some sort of inside knowledge about it. Could men be witches too? Gran said we got our powers when we started going through 'the change', and as far as I was aware men didn't have a menopause to speak of. They just got rid of their first wives, started dating a twenty-year-old and bought a power boat or a sports car.

That's what Jack had done, wasn't it?

"Thanks for checking on me," I smiled.

"Anytime, Tess. Let me know if you need anything."

Considering that Jack had a friend in the Kettle Harbor Police Department that seemed all too happy to let me take the blame for this murder rather than consider that his golf buddy might have done it, I would need a miracle. "I will," I replied, then set off towards the care home.

CHAPTER 11

Shaded Wood had a somber energy when I stepped inside. The staff seemed to be operating at half speed, walking without really lifting their feet off the ground or talking above a mumble. The air conditioning unit closest to me was humming, with the occasional *thump thump* that older units did that made you think that there was a good chance it might fall off the wall and crush you to death.

Despite the cool air, I was sweaty. I wasn't sure if it was because of the walk over here from the beach, the nervous sweat that you could reasonably expect when you step into the workplace of a woman that people think you murdered, or if it was a hot flush. It was probably a combination of all three.

"Tess," Chris said, lifting up a hand in a half-hearted wave from behind the nurse's station. I watched as he got to his feet, walked through the door and came out onto the main floor of the day room.

"Hi," I replied. I wasn't really sure what to say, I had assumed I could walk in here to ask a few questions but hadn't considered the reality that they would all be in total shock about it. "How's it been around here today? I can't even imagine…"

"It's been strange. Casey had only been here a few months, but the residents liked her, she was friendly and seemed to really enjoy her job. Well, *most* of the time, but everyone has their rough patches," he said, turning his palms upwards in a *'I don't know what else to say'* gesture.

There was a thud, followed by a strange squeaking sound. We both turned to the window that usually looked out over the back lawns. It was floor to ceiling, it meant that if you were in a wheelchair, you were still able to have an unrestricted view of the gardens. Not today though. The view was very much restricted by the full-frontal display of Lionel who was once again completely naked. The squeak was the sound of body parts sliding across the glass, I won't mention which parts because I hope to forget that I ever saw them.

Chris let out a small chuckle, "Lionel actually said this was a protest, that he wouldn't get dressed again until the police caught the killer. In his mind I'm sure he thinks this is the equivalent of a political prisoner's hunger strike."

"It's nice that he is so free with his body, I guess," I smiled. The front door to the building opened and a man stepped inside, his face was ghostly pale with deep, dark circles under both eyes. I glanced quickly at Chris to make sure I wasn't the only one that could see this guy, he looked eerily similar to my grandmother who was an actual ghost.

"I could have put money on it…" Chris muttered under his breath.

"Honey, not today," Louise called to the man in the doorway. "It's not the time today, your grandmother knows the score, you can't be here. We told you it was two weeks."

"Please don't make me leave! I need to be close to her," he whimpered. Close to who, his grandma? I scanned the room and found a disgruntled, grey-haired woman who looked like the type of person that would pop a child's ball if it came over the fence into her yard.

"Don't make me call for security again, Bobby," Louise said, rising to her feet and lifting the receiver of the desk phone.

"Okay, Okay," Bobby replied, holding up his hands and taking a few steps backwards. He gave a look to his grandmother who dismissively swiped a hand through the air; she didn't seem to want him here either. Bobby looked at Louise who was moving a finger down to the numbers on the phone in slow-motion, a threat that he better hurry up and leave before she pushed one of them and got a guard in here. Then he looked at Chris and I, his eyes locked with mine and then he suddenly looked down at his feet before disappearing through the door.

With Bobby gone, the occupants of the day room could get back to their previous activity of staring at me and muttering to who ever they were sat next to.

"Who was that?" I asked.

Chris opened his mouth to speak, but simultaneously lifted his left wrist towards his face and checked the time on his watch. "He's a— oh, you know I've actually got a session with a resident right now. Maybe we could grab a coffee tomorrow or something, if you're free."

"A coffee?" I repeated. Did he mean grab a coffee, or *grab a coffee?* My eye flicked to the wedding ring on his left hand again and I felt as if someone had let the air out of my balloon. "I don't know." He followed my line of sight and saw what I was looking at, weirdly his expression seemed to match my own.

"I'm not… it's not what you think. I don't have time to explain it all right now, I'm already running late. The Coffee Cup on Barksdale, ten o'clock tomorrow morning. Is that good?"

"Well—"

"Great! See you then!" he smiled. Before I could figure out if I'd actually agreed to that or not, he'd jogged down the corridor and into a treatment room.

How could a gold band on his left ring finger *not* be what I think? I don't want to be going on a date with a married man, although no one actually used the word 'date' and curiosity alone would be enough to get me to show up. Should I judge a man for asking me out if I'm currently a person-off-interest in a murder investigation? Did he even ask me out? Well at least I wasn't overthinking it.

"Tess?" Louise called out. She was no longer behind the nurse's station desk, at some point during my internal conversation she'd walked over to me. "Everything okay?"

"Yeah. It's been a weird day…"

"Tell me about it," she scoffed. "Why ain't your sister on this? We had that creep with the porn-moustache in here earlier asking questions and he didn't seem all that interested in the answers."

"Steve?"

"Is that his name? He looks like he should be on a watchlist."

"Michelle can't work the case because—"

"Because they think you did it?" she guessed. "That's bull, you're a smart woman, ain't no way you're killing somebody where you work and leaving the body in your own pool. That's what a dumb person would do. I said as much to porn-stache, but he didn't have his listening ears switched on."

"Yeah, he's already made up his mind, so I don't get the impression that he's really looking for information unless it points to me," I replied.

"See, I hate that. I hate people taking short cuts at their jobs. I'm all for 'work smart, not hard', but there's got to be a limit. I can't decide to just skip parts of my job that suck because I'm taking care of people, porn-stache is supposed to be looking for someone dangerous, and that ain't you!"

"What was it you tried to tell him that he didn't listen to?" I asked. I felt a heat in my hands, I glanced down and noticed a slight glow around my fingers so quickly made fists to hide them. Louise paused for a second, then a glow of the same color flashed in her eyes. A slight golden hue radiated out from her iris, and then she continued.

"Well Bobby is a problem, that's for sure. And then there's… you know what, let's take a seat," she said, gesturing behind me to the chairs by the window where my dad usually sat. "Bingo," she smiled, answering a question I hadn't verbalized, *'where was he?'* "Never misses a game."

He often presented his bingo winnings when I'd visit on a Monday, typically they included some sort of body lotion and a huge chunk of fruit cake – which he would then share with me.

We sat down, grateful that Lionel was no longer pressing his plums against the glass closest to us. He was now lay down on the lawn about a hundred yards away, still exposing his body to the elements of course.

"Bobby is a problem, has been for a while now," she began, keeping her voice barely above a whisper. "Took a real shine to Casey when she started here, started bringing gifts for her and trying to give her notes. His grandma has been living here for years now, and he used to only really come round on her birthday. Now? Pfft... every dang day. He likes lurking in the corridors, eavesdropping and such. We said to him that he needed to stop giving her things like that at work, but he interpreted that as *'stop giving her things inside the building she works.'"*

"He had flowers the other day," I said, remembering the old woman yelling at him about it.

"Oh yeah, and I said to him that he had a two week ban from coming onto the premises, *including* the parking lot. You know he started leaving stuff on her windshield? He would wait by her car when she got off shift and it really freaked her out." There'd been a rose under her wiper on Friday, I'd assumed it was from Jack. Did that mean Bobby was still trying to get to her despite Louise's ban?

"And Steve didn't want to listen to any of that?"

"Sure didn't. He spoke to me and Chris. I bet we said the exact same thing, too. She was new here, so it wasn't like we got much time to get to know her. She knew Liam already from somewhere else, I don't know if you met him much," she said. I shrugged. "Those two were close, so I said to porn-stache to ask him some questions because maybe he knew something. I know he was invited to the engagement party so maybe he saw something."

I leaned back in the chair and let out a sigh. Outside I could see Lionel on his feet, now standing in warrior pose. Louise caught sight of him and whatever strange hold my magic had on her seemed to lessen.

"He is gonna catch his death out there, how many times have I said it...?" she muttered, then looking back at me. "Tess? What were we just talking about?"

"Bingo," I replied.

Lionel shifted from one yoga position to another, although it was a pose I hadn't seen before that seemed to involve a lot of thrusting. "Oh hell no," Louise tutted, "He's gonna learn today, I ain't— sorry Tess, I've gotta deal with that."

"Sure," I nodded. Louise headed for the door out to the back lawn, and I looked back out of the window to see Lionel as he heard the door open. He swiftly broke out into a full sprint as Louise yelled at him across the grass. He was surprisingly spry.

My stomach rumbled, a reminder that I'd yet to feed myself today. I pulled out my phone to see if Michelle had given me any more information about tonight's event. I had one message that simply said, *'Books and Such on Centre St, eleven o'clock. Bring wine.'*

I walked out of Shaded Wood and round to the parking lot. It wasn't until I was standing among the sea of cars that I remembered that I'd walked here, meaning that I would also have to walk home. I felt a throb of pain in my ankle as if in protest at the amount of movement I'd already put it through. Then I noticed Bobby, he was hunched over and sobbing onto the hood of a car, *Casey's* car.

Why would her car be here? She'd been at her engagement party last night, not at work. I had a million things that I needed to run by Michelle when I saw her, none of which was related to magic. Bobby started to wail loudly, and I backed away from the parking lot and made my way round to the front of the building and onto the sidewalk.

Casey had been arguing with Jack, she had bruises on her body, she was being stalked at work and appeared to have driven here from her own engagement party. I planned to head home before I was due at the bookstore, there was no way I was wandering the streets until eleven o'clock. The tide was high, the salty air mixed with the smell of sea food from the plethora of ocean-themed restaurants. My stomach rumbled again.

I passed 'Burger Shack' on the corner of Pine and Bridge Street, I stopped in my tracks as melted cheese and chargrilled beef lured me inside. I nearly bumped into the man walking out at the same time that I was entering. I was about to apologize – even though it was mostly his fault – and he made a second attempt to barge past me, his shoulder colliding with mine as he left with a bundle of hot food in his arms.

I caught sight of his face; it was the man that had been comforting Casey at Shaded Wood a few days ago, the same man that had escorted dad to the hotel on Friday night. Where was he going in such a hurry?

CHAPTER 12

After a tactical power nap at home, I had ventured back out of my house and was now standing in front of Books and Such. Luckily it was a short walk from my front door to the bookstore, and it was along well lit roads. Kettle Harbor was typically such a safe town but knowing that there was a killer on the loose I wondered if maybe I should have exercised a little more caution before travelling solo after dark.

The store was on the corner, the entrance was built onto an angled wall where the two streets met, and I stared at the blacked out windows with confusion. Hadn't this been the place we were supposed to meet? It looked like it was closed up and that no one was inside. I stepped closer to the door, pressing my face against the glass window built into it and holding my right hand over my brow to block out the streetlight so I could look for movement.

"It is open, Theresa," a voice announced. I flinched and clutched my chest, only then noticing the ghostly figure of my grandmother stood to my left.

"Women can have heart attacks too, you know? People think it just affects men but I'm telling you, it's more common than you think. It's gonna be pretty messed up if you scare me to death."

"I thought you heard me appear, my mistake. Anyway, as I was saying, the door is open. Just walk inside, they are waiting for you," she smiled.

"What am I walking into? Is this like a cult or something? It's not that I don't trust Michelle, but do you remember that time she joined an MLM? I wouldn't be surprised if I got in there and she's got another box full of crappy lipsticks or essential oils that you rub into your eyeballs."

"They were for rubbing into your *temples* if I recall correctly, but tonight is not a sales pitch. This is an opportunity for you to meet with local witches, they will be an important part of your life from now on," she nodded.

I reached for the handle but didn't open the door. Once I stepped into this place and saw everyone else then I was acknowledging that this was all real, *really* acknowledging it. It's one thing to become delusional by yourself, but doing it in a group of people? Cult! Jeez, you never think you'll be dumb enough to get suckered into one of these things.

I turned the handle and stepped inside. I was almost blinded by the light, squinting up at the bulbs in the ceiling that hadn't been visible from the street. It wasn't dark and empty in here, there were five women sat in a circle and they were all well-lit.

I spotted Lena first, she stood up and put her arm around my shoulder to guide me to an empty chair. "It's a privacy spell," she said.

"Stops people from poking their noses into our business," Michelle added. I sat down and looked at the gathered women, as well as my sister and Lena, there was also the woman from the dry cleaner's, Lisa, and Louise. My mouth hung open.

"You… you're a…" I managed.

"Witch?" Louise laughed.

"But—"

"Oh, I know you used a little magic on me earlier, but only because I let you! I know you're hunting for a killer so there's no use in anybody keeping secrets. I think Bobby is creepy as hell, I don't need to be under the influence of any spell to tell you that much," she exclaimed.

"Lisa?" I said, turning my head.

"Surprise!" she smiled, laughing nervously.

A cork popped and the woman from the dry-cleaning place started pouring champagne into six flutes that were hovering in the air in front of her. Once each glass was filled it floated into the hands of each witch sat in the circle, including me. I opened my hand to catch the stem before it collided with my body and covered me in liquid.

"To Tess!" Lena cheered, raising her glass. The others lifted theirs, and I sat there like a deer in the headlights. I started to remember all the times I'd said to Lena that I thought something weird was going on at the hotel and she'd brushed it off as if I was hallucinating. She'd be hearing about that again, that's for sure.

"When can I ask what's going on?" I asked.

"Drink first, questions later," Michelle replied.

"I have a lot of questions so it would make sense to start now, wouldn't it?"

Lena tipped every last drop of champagne into her mouth and then turned to me, "welcome to the club! I feel like I've been waiting forever to tell you what's *really* going on around here."

"Which is?"

"That Kettle Harbor is due a demon invasion at any minute? Or maybe that the dead don't always stay dead? Or that I'm pretty sure there's a vampire lurking around here now?" the dry-cleaning woman huffed.

As if able to sense that I didn't know the woman's name, my grandmother's ghost appeared by my side and spoke, "Kathleen, try to avoid frightening the girl."

"Girl? I'm forty-two," I mumbled.

"How long have you known about this world exactly? Just over twelve hours?" my grandmother scowled. "As I said, this meeting is supposed to be an introduction to the community and not an opportunity for you to peddle your theories about vampires…again."

"It ain't a theory, there's been animal attacks in them woods

Linda," Louise added, using my grandmother's first name as if they were old friends. "They've been coming in that hospital with the blood drained right out of 'em and the doctors ain't none the wiser."

"It's true," Lena added, "I've seen it myself."

"I see…" Gran replied.

"I can't believe my little sister is all grown up!" Michelle said, holding out her champagne flute for Kathleen to refill.

"Again, forty-two."

"I am sure you are all aware that a potential was murdered last night. Casey Quinn was killed and left in the pool at Moody Moon, putting Theresa at the top of the suspect list as far as the police are concerned," my grandmother began.

"Not *all* the police, just one officer in particular," Michelle added, "and he doesn't know his ass from his elbow."

"Stupid people can still be dangerous, Michelle. Even more so, in fact!"

"Yeah, Steve has it out for me and I'm pretty sure he's ignoring evidence at this point. Scott said you heard yelling at Jack's house," I said, directing my comment at Lisa, "that you called the cops and that nothing came of it."

"Yes, a man with a seventies pornstar moustache showed up and went into the house for about an hour. He came out again with a Tupperware box of leftovers and he smelled like tiramisu," Lisa replied.

"You sniffed him?" Kathleen grimaced.

"No, not up close at least. I have a good sense of smell that's all. It's why I can't stand being out on the boats with Scott when he has that bucket of chum for the fish. I'd rather flush my own head down the toilet because honestly it wouldn't smell as bad," Lisa said, almost gagging at the thought.

"I have never known a group so unable to stay focused in my life, or death," gran complained. "As I was saying, Casey Quinn was murdered – not by a vampire, Kathleen before you even *think* of interrupting me with that suggestion."

"Strangled, Gran," Michelle clarified.

"Let me lay it all out for you because I've been pretty busy this afternoon," I said, hoping to steer them in the right direction. "Casey was seen arguing with a man in the alley behind O'Malley's last night and she had bruises on her wrist and temple earlier in the week as if she's gone through the wringer. Given that you called the police about her and Jack yelling at each other, Lisa, it would suggest that this is some sort of escalation of domestic abuse."

"You really think Jack strangled her and then tried to pin it on you?" Michelle asked. "I'm not saying that's not what happened, but… I mean you were married to the guy for a long time, Tess. Do you really think he's capable of that?"

"You don't know who she was arguing with behind O'Malley's?" Louise asked.

"No, just that it was a man. That's all Finn could tell me," I shrugged.

"Of course it was a man, it's always a man," she huffed.

"Were you working last night, Louise?"

"You betcha! They've gotta put a woman like me on shift on a Saturday night because if somebody *this* fine was let loose on a weekend then who knows what might happen?!" she laughed.

"Was Casey there?"

"On the night of her engagement party? Hell no! She had better things to be doing that dealing with Lionel's naked old ass running about the place." Louise held out her champagne flute towards Kathleen who begrudgingly stood up and poured from the bottle once more.

"You are all more than capable of doing this yourselves you know, I'm the oldest one here! You should all be waiting on me hand and foot!" she grumbled.

"Are we getting round to the ritual any time soon or should we pick this up again tomorrow?" Lisa asked. "I've got a documentary about D.B. Cooper being recorded tonight but I'd rather watch it when it goes out because Scott will be talking about it tomorrow and he'll spoil it."

"Spoiler alert: they don't know who D.B. Cooper is," Louise tutted.

Lisa looked briefly annoyed, but Kathleen refilled her glass once more and peace was restored.

"Can I just get back to Casey?" I asked, "her car was in the parking lot behind Shaded Wood, when was she last there?"

"Friday," Louise replied. "She was all upset about something; Liam was trying to calm her down for…well it must have been almost an hour. I sent her home because being one person short is manageable but being *two* people down is hard work. I saw her drive off the lot and then Liam got back to work, *kinda.*"

"And you told Steve to speak to Liam?" I asked.

"Hello? Ritual?" Lisa prodded.

"Tess," Michelle said, rising to her feet and holding her champagne flute aloft, "do you swear to honor the witches the came before you, and the witches that will come after?"

"What?"

"Just say yes, Theresa," Gran said, motioning as if she were about to nudge me with her elbow but instead sending a chill over my entire body as her arm passed through me.

"Yes," I replied.

"Will you aid the cause?" Michelle continued.

"What cause?"

"The *cause*, Tess," Michelle huffed.

"I have absolutely no idea what you're talking about."

"We protect this town from darkness and danger," Kathleen added. "I'm talking warlocks, werewolves, witch hunters, and VAMPIRES!"

"It's just sort of a 'you watch my back, I'll watch yours' sort of deal," Michelle clarified. "Like a neighborhood watch, but we've got magic. I mean, those are the rules for our little group anyway."

"Is this a coven?" I asked.

"Officially, we're a book club," Lisa answered. "We agreed that the word 'coven' makes you think of wrinkled old hags with warty noses and hunched backs that eat children. We mostly drink and read steamy romance books."

"Do you agree to aid the cause or not, Tess?" Michelle repeated.

"Sure, whatever. If it's a neighborhood watch type of deal then I'm in, because there's a real killer out there and I need all the help I can get to find them."

"You gotta drink," Louise said. The five of them were now standing and the glasses in their hands had turned to gold chalices, as had the one I was holding. I peered inside and the champagne had been replaced with a deep red liquid.

"Is this blood?" I winced.

"It's red wine. Would you prefer it if it *was* blood? Because that could mean you're a—" Kathleen began.

"Enough about vampires!" Gran yelled. "Drink the wine, Theresa. It will allow you to access the powers you are entitled to." As I looked into the chalice again, I could see that the wine was emitting a slight glow, a dark light spiraled inside it as if I were swirling it around.

"To Tess!" Michelle said once more. All six of us drank simultaneously, and I felt a heat as it passed my lips and trickled down my throat. I felt my cheeks flush in the way they always did with wine, my lips tingled, and I felt lightheaded almost immediately.

"Did you just drink the whole thing?" Louise asked. "Oh honey, that stuff is like sixty percent proof, it's harder than vodka. We were all just sipping on it, you're gonna need carrying home."

"I can't feel my tongue," I muttered. "My hands feel fizzy."

"Kathleen!" Gran snapped.

"Hey, it's not my fault she can't handle her liquor. Don't blame me for this. I'll get her a cab, don't get your panties in a twist," Kathleen laughed.

"I do not wear pant— Michelle, do something!"

"She's fine, Gran. Don't you remember what it felt like when you got full access to your powers? The wine takes the edge off, although she's drank enough to take *all* the edges off, she's now just a sphere," Michelle laughed.

The conversation seemed to continue around me as I slumped into my chair, my vision hazy as I looked at the faces of the weird little group I was now a part of. Kathleen stood up and started to read a passage from a book and I noticed that the others all had copies of it too, was this *really* a book club? I couldn't see the front cover well enough to know what they were talking about.

At some point I was ushered into a taxi, Michelle climbed in next to me, and the engine rumbled beneath us. My arms felt heavy, and my fingers were almost itchy as if there was something underneath the skin. Michelle told me that it would 'wear off soon', but that provided little comfort. It was like every thought was clouded, all I could think about was Casey and her body being left in the hotel pool.

By the time I was in bed – with a lot of assistance from my sister – I felt as if I could almost hear Casey's voice in my ear. It was barely above a whisper, and I couldn't be sure that it wasn't the giant chalice of wine talking, but it sounded like her calling out to me. *'Help me, Tess.'*

CHAPTER 13

*H*angovers in your forties are nothing like the ones from your twenties. I could stay out with Lena until three or four in the morning, doing shots and dancing until we could dance no more, then wake up the next day feeling fresh as a daisy and ready for another full day of being a functional adult. That wasn't happening today, though. Today I opened my eyes and wondered if I'd fallen down the stairs at some point last night.

My ankle felt freshly injured, as if no time had passed since I stumbled over a pothole during the half-marathon. I could feel my pulse throbbing offensively in my temples, the sound of blood moving around my brain felt *loud* and as if my body was trying to punish me for some reason. It was like a cry for help, as if my cells had all teamed up to demand I nourish them with water and vegetables.

"How's your head?" Michelle asked. She was likely speaking at a totally acceptable volume, but it hit my ear drums as if she were screaming through a megaphone.

"I'm dying," I whispered back. Part of the magic of whispering is that once you say something in a hushed voice, the other person typically reciprocates by replying in a similar way. Not *my* sister, however.

"You can't die until you've cleared your name, Tess. So get up," she insisted, *louder* than she'd spoken a moment earlier. If I survived this hangover I would make sure to retaliate at some point. Michelle stepped further into my bedroom and revealed that she was carrying a breakfast tray loaded with everything my body was desperate for; a giant glass of fresh orange juice, a second glass filled with water, and a breakfast burrito wrapped in the branded paper from Burger Shack.

I brought the water to my lips and with three huge gulps I emptied the entire glass. Instantly the pounding in my head receded, my vision no longer blurring with every beat of my heart. I flexed my ankle, rotating my foot to test the joint – it was pain free.

"What is this?" I asked, staring at the empty glass in my hand.

"Do you think you're the first witch to get wasted in that bookstore?" she laughed. "I developed a little spell to undo the effects of that wine because Kathleen has been making extra strong batches lately and we all still have jobs to go to after those meetings. Have you ever been to the dry-cleaners and she was just slumped over behind the counter with sunglasses on her face? That's why."

"I see." I tore the paper off the burrito and took a huge bite. This wasn't magic in the same way that the water clearly was but had it's own unique healing qualities. "How often do you have those meetings?" I asked.

"Every week, technically. It's a book club and sometimes we haven't managed to read the book in time, when that happens we just get together and chat anyway. Kathleen loves ranting about vampires and how dangerous they are, but which book do you think she picked last week? Twilight. I bet you ten bucks she's written her own fanfiction about it."

"But didn't you guys say there is actually a vampire here, Lena said she's seen patients in the hospital with bites and—"

"Just finish your breakfast, we can worry about vampires another time," she said, cutting me off. "I'm at the station most of today, I wanted to make sure you were doing okay before I left."

"Yeah, I guess I've got some reading to do," I gestured to the books still scattered on my bedroom floor. "Does Gran just show up whenever? Can you *summon* her?"

"She's not a demon, Tess. You don't summon ghosts, not ones like her anyway. She just pops up at the least convenient moments, it's like her party trick." Michelle hopped off the bed and with a snap of her fingers replaced her loungewear set with her police uniform, her hair pulled back into a tight bun beneath her hat. My mouth hung open in shock for a second, but then I remembered I had a mouthful of food and didn't want to spill scrambled egg all over the bed sheets.

"If Jack shows up here again, call me. If you think you have a lead, don't do anything insane – just call me. If you realize that you are actually the killer and start to feel murderous rage bubble up inside you again – call me!" she grinned.

"Don't you have somewhere to be?" I grumbled. She continued laughing as she left the room, raced down the stairs and disappeared through my front door. A quick look at the clock on my nightstand informed me that it was almost nine o'clock. I leaned back against the pillows and closed my eyes as I continued to chew, savoring the flavors and contemplating what I was going to do with my day, slowly breathing in through my— *oh crap!* I was supposed to meet Chris in an hour!

I gasped and inhaled Pico de Gallo which caused me to cough and wheeze. Was I choking? I could hardly perform the Heimlich maneuver on myself, why did I have to wait until I was single to choke on a breakfast food? Was this going to be my final thought? *Damn tomato.* Michelle only just left! My timing sucked. I was going to die in my bed all by myself because I couldn't chew my food properly, like a toddler.

As my internal monologue continued to chastise me, the coughing managed to dislodge the errant item and I was able to breath normally again.

"Theresa, you are supposed to chew each mouthful adequately so as to avoid unnecessary risks like that," my grandmother said, suddenly appearing at the foot of the bed in a cloud of *judgmental* smoke. "From what I gather, twenty chews are required to—"

"Is that helpful? It's like showing up curbside as someone's house is burning down and telling them to keep an eye on their candles," I huffed.

"I take your point," she nodded. "I was curious as to whether you might be interested in using some magic to make yourself presentable before your date."

She had always been a well-spoken woman, taking care to select each word and constructing a sentence as if she'd fallen out of a Jane Austen novel. She despised abbreviations for some reason. Why? No one knows. I'd asked her about it more than once, but she always just said that there was always enough time to speak properly. I would roll my eyes progressively harder every time I got that reply.

"It's not a date. He said he had something to explain to me and he was busy with the residents yesterday so he just suggested coffee because he had some free time outside of work to—"

"The gentleman in question has requested your company *outside* of the place you typically run into each other. He is utilizing his free time to interact with you in a setting that does not pertain to his role as your father's physiotherapist. This seems like a date to me, and it would serve you well to look less like you crawled out of your own grave this morning when you arrive," she said.

I got off the bed and walked over to the full-length mirror at the other side of the room. Michelle's magic water might have helped with the internal consequences of all the wine I drank last night, but it had done absolutely nothing for my face. Dehydration deepened every wrinkle around my eyes, the lines from the outside of my nose to the corners of my mouth looked as if they'd been carved into place, my skin was blotchy and my cheeks had deep hollows that gave me a slight skeletal look.

By skeletal I of course mean that I looked like death, not that I'd turned into some waif like Kate Moss. The silvers in my hair usually blended in with the ashy blonde surrounding them, but now stood out like they were producing their own light.

It was like I'd aged overnight. It was the first time I'd ever looked into a mirror and felt like there was an old woman staring back.

"Magic can fix this?" I grumbled.

"Fix? There is nothing to fix, Theresa. You are not broken; you are simply aging. Old is the goal, remember? No one wants to die young. You simply did not keep yourself adequately hydrated and this has resulted in you shriveling slightly, like a raisin. I would recommend another glass of water or two before you go off indulging in coffee with your new beau. That will take some time to reach the skin, however, so I recommend a little magical boost in the interim."

"Okay, what do I need to do?" I asked.

Gran talked me through a breathing exercise that allowed me to clear my mind, it probably took longer than normal as I was in a semi-panic about my old-lady face and catastrophizing that I was totally past it. Kylie Minogue is fifty-four, that is twelve entire years older than I am and she looks better than I did in college. What is her secret? Was she a witch too?

During a brief window when I managed to silence my inner critic, Gran told me to ball up my fists and *will* myself to be ready for the day. I closed my eyes and felt the sensation of my skin plumping slightly around my mouth and eyes, a warm tingle as cleanser and moisturizer slathered themselves over my cheeks. There was mounting heat in my hands as if I were holding a match that was burning to its end.

"Can I stop now?" I asked, "I don't think I'm doing this right, should it hurt?"

"It is like training a muscle, you get stronger the more you use it," she replied. "But I would say that you can open your eyes now." I released the tension in my hands, flexing my fingers over and over until the aching stopped. I looked in the mirror; the hands of time hadn't been wound backwards, but I didn't look like I'd been on an all-night binge-drinking session now – that was what I had been hoping for.

My face looked a little more full, the lines around my eyes not quite so deep, and it looked as though I'd added a light coverage foundation, some bronzer in the right places to give me the illusion of cheek-bones, and mascara. Make-up sat differently on my face than it used to, gathering in the creases and sweating off my forehead when a hot flush would strike. For a first foray into practicing magic I'd give myself top marks.

"Your first date," Gran smiled.

"I've been on dates before… and this isn't a date."

"You have only ever stepped out with Jack Stevens and considering how that turned out, you may as well wipe the slate clean and start over," she added.

"Are you even going to comment on the fact that I just did actual magic? On purpose? I didn't just accidentally freeze anybody or zap myself across the harbor, I thought of something I wanted to do and made it happen?!"

"A student is only ever as good as their teacher," she winked. "Now step to it! Being late for your first date is a bad idea."

"It's not—"

"Go!"

* * *

I walked past the bakery on Barksdale as I had a thousand times before, but this time there was a knot in my stomach that I couldn't shake. I was nervous. When was the last time I'd felt like that? I wasn't nervous in the police station yesterday morning, not really. I'd been afraid that I was about to get in big trouble for something I hadn't done, but nerves didn't really come into it.

I'd felt apprehensive when I'd first stepped into Moody Moon with the keys in my hand, I'd felt the cocktail of excitement and concern that most people must experience when they are embarking on a new career path. But stepping into The Coffee Place I found myself trying to take slow breaths so as not to chicken out and run home.

This *wasn't* a date. Chris had a wedding ring, he was a married man. He said he had something to 'explain', but I wasn't about to be taken for an idiot. I knew what it felt like to find out your husband was fooling around with someone else, I wasn't about to be that 'someone else' for another woman. So why was I here?

"Tess?" Chris called. He'd secured a table in the corner and judging by the level of the liquid in his coffee cup, he'd been here a while. Was I late? I gave him a nod of acknowledgement, then felt my 'fight or flight' response kick in. *Get out of there, go!*

"I'll just order," I said, forcing my feet to carry me to the counter and not make a break for it through the front door.

"Good morning, what can I getcha?" A young man wearing a black polo shirt lifted a finger in preparation to punch my order into his little computer screen.

"Coffee. Black. Strong."

"Any creamer? Sugar? Milk? Syrups? We've got cookies, too. Pastries?" he continued.

"Coffee. Black. Strong. Hot," I clarified.

"Coming up. I can bring it over," he smiled, jerking his head towards Chris who was still on his feet in case I forgot where he was sitting. I hadn't. I paid for my drink, then shuffled across the floor tiles.

The things I saw during my nursing career would send most people into therapy. I have seen things inserted into every imaginable place, I have seen injuries that even Stephen King could not envision, and yet *now* I found myself keen to look away.

"I got here early," Chris offered, holding out my chair. "I didn't want to be late." I sat down and realized that my slow, steady inhalations were now capturing his cologne. It was intoxicating, the scent of a man that had yet to totally screw me over; what a novelty.

"Me neither," I replied. He wasn't wearing his uniform, instead he was in a navy-blue Henley shirt that had the top two buttons open. It really spoke to how unflattering the bright lighting was in the day room at Shaded Wood, because sat across the table from me I was able to really take in what he looked like.

He cradled his coffee cup, his wedding ring making a *'clink'* sound as it hit the ceramic. I felt my stomach flip, and my posture seemed to deflate noticeably enough for him to respond, "so I told you I would explain."

"You did," I nodded, bracing for impact. A loud group entered, talking at a volume that would suggest they were all hard of hearing. I glared at them for a moment, then turned back to Chris who seemed to have a nervous energy that could rival my own. "Why don't we go for a walk? I'll get them to put my coffee in a to-go cup and we can get some fresh air," I suggested.

He leaned back in his chair and I saw his expression soften, "sounds good to me."

I went over to the counter to change my order and silently prayed that Chris wasn't about to confess that he was the one that killed Casey. Of course he hadn't, right? It was a stupid, invasive thought that decided to pop into my head at the worst possible moment. But now I couldn't get rid of the idea.

CHAPTER 14

$\mathcal{W}$e walked along Barksdale until it curved around towards the shore and became Bridge Street. I wasn't sure what he was waiting for exactly, he hadn't spoken since we stepped outside The Coffee Place and I wonder just how bad the revelation was about to be. Why did he need to psych himself up so much?

"I'm just gonna ask, because if I don't I'm not sure you're gonna tell me and honestly I feel like I'm too old for mind games. Are you married? You look married. You have the ring and all, I used to have one of those you know," I blurted. "I mean, I'm not married now. You know I got divorced, right? It's a classic 'girl meets boy, girl falls in love, girl kind of puts herself on the back burner for 20 years and then finds out he's been cheating on her.'"

We walked past whale watch, crossing the street so that we were close to the wall separating the town from the sand. He stopped, stepping into my path slightly so that I was forced to stop too. "She died."

"Who? Casey?"

"My... my wife died. It's been almost two years and I've not known what to do with myself since it happened, but we had a daughter, so completely falling apart wasn't an option. I still had to show up to work, pay bills, make sure we had health insurance and all that awful responsible stuff that you need to do when you're a parent," he explained. He was looking at his shoes as if fearful of what I would say.

I reached out a hand and wrapped it around one of his, prompting him to look up. "I'm sorry," I offered.

"I wear the ring because it stops people asking questions, you know? We used to live further out, we moved closer to the center after... when it was just the two of us. I got the job at Shaded Wood and I guess I spotted an opportunity to not have to talk about what happened every day. At my old job I would get *the look*, you know the look don't you?"

"I do. I was in nurse for a long time, Chris, I've given the look more times than I can count."

"I know," he nodded. I realized I was still holding his hand, the breeze rolling over the ocean was catching his cologne and causing it to spiral around me.

"I went to the hotel launch and I was hoping to have more time to speak to you, but then your friend came in and she saw the ring and I saw the look in her eyes— I owed you an explanation at that point and I guess I've just been trying to build up the nerve to tell you the truth."

"What did you want to speak to me about?" I asked. He squeezed my hand and offered me a smile that barely moved his lips, but made his eyes sparkle and I felt a heat wash over me as he held me in his gaze. Not heat like a hot flush, and not the heat for my newly acquired powers, but that warmth when you feel like you're on the precipice of something life altering.

"I need to preface this whole thing by saying that I don't know if I'm ready, and I know that it's a lot for me to put on you and you're more than welcome to tell me to go to hell, but I would like to spend more time with you. I want to talk to you about things that aren't your dad's joint mobility, or Lionel's plums," he said, grinning broadly as I started to laugh. "You have familial responsibilities, and so do I, and we've both worked in healthcare, and you're beautiful, and I find myself searching for more things to say to you every time we meet because I don't want the conversation to end. Like now, I'm rambling now because you're not saying anything, and I want this to keep going."

"Beautiful?" I repeated. He nodded and squeezed my hand a little tighter. "So it would be an experiment, we'd both be dragging decades worth of baggage into this and it might be a complete disaster but you're asking if I want to risk disaster with you?"

"Yes," he confirmed.

I wanted to soak in the feeling but a patrol car rolled by and I saw Steve glaring out of the driver seat as he passed us. Like a reflex, I dropped Chris's hand. "Sorry I just—"

"It's fine," he assured me.

"Were you at work on Saturday night?" I asked, "I know it's a conversational U-Turn but I'm trying to piece together a few things."

"Yeah I was there from mid-afternoon. Why?"

"Did you happen to see Casey there? Or see her car?" I pressed.

"She wasn't working Saturday. The last time I saw her was Friday afternoon," he replied.

"But her car..." I sighed.

"Well she'd been giving Liam a ride to work the last week or so, his battery died or something and he was saving up to get a new one. I can't remember if he was scheduled to be in or not, I don't remember seeing him either though."

A car engine grew louder as it rumbled past us; the same patrol car as before. Steve wanted me to feel watched, he wanted me to know that he wasn't letting me off the hook. Everyone was right, he did have a stupid porn moustache. He narrowed his eyes as he slowed down, lowering the window to speak.

"The plot thickens," he grunted.

"What plot?" I asked. He killed the engine and stepped out of the car, tucking his thumbs into his belt as he walked around the hood to stand a few feet away from Chris and I.

"Do you wanna know what I think?" he said.

"Not even a little," I muttered.

"I think you had been plotting your revenge for a long time, I think you were just waiting for an opportunity to strike out at the woman that wronged you. You didn't want there to be another Mrs. Stevens, you didn't want them to have their happy ending. We know you've been tracking her movements."

"I have *not* been—"

"We know all about it. Matter of fact, I'm starting to see just how many things you've been lying about. I've got eyes and ears all over this—" Steve continued talking as my attention drifted to the ghost of my grandmother who was sat in the passenger seat of the patrol car. She was leaning forward and it looked as if she was doing something with her hands that I couldn't quite see. Seconds later the car alarm was blasting out so loudly that birds took flight.

I suppressed a laugh, and out of the corner of my eye I could see that Chris had done the same. While Steve dived back into the car to deal with the offending sound, Chris and I continued our walk along the sidewalk – this time a little quicker.

"For what it's worth, I think that man is stupid," Chris offered.

"He's friends with my ex-husband. They're just looking for someone to blame and I fit the bill, that's all. I would say that I'm trying not to take it personally, but that would be a lie," I shrugged. "I was nowhere near the hotel on Saturday night." Chris's phone started beeping in his jeans pocket and when he pulled it out to look at the screen his face twisted into a grimace.

"Sorry, I've gotta take this," he said, stepping away to speak.

I looked back down the street and could just about see Steve kicking the side of the patrol car that was *still* screaming. I took a sip from my cardboard coffee cup and leaned against the wall to look out at the island. If Lena had stayed with me then I would have had an alibi. I mean, I did technically have an alibi, but I doubted Steve would be willing to sit down with a ghost and hear out her side of things.

"That was Louise, she's short staffed again so wanted to know if I could come in early to help her ratios. I think she just wants someone else to chase Lionel around for a few hours," Chris explained.

"Well I've just got to keep pushing forward at the hotel as if I might still get to properly open this weekend, I haven't been back there since yesterday so I don't even know if I can get into the building."

"Why don't I walk with you, it's basically next door to where I'm headed."

"Okay," I agreed.

"I can bombard you with questions if you like."

"Is it one-way, or are we taking turns?"

"Depends how much time we have?" he smiled. "Okay, first question—"

"I feel like I'm on a gameshow."

"What made you go into nursing in the first place?" he asked.

"My mom was a veterinarian. Sometimes she'd take Michelle and I to work after she'd finished for the day just so we could hang out with the animals that were in overnight. I liked the idea of helping animals and I guess that was something I was interested in for a while but then…" I trailed off, not wanting to finish the thought, at least not truthfully. "I just figured helping humans would be equally satisfying, so I went down that route. What about you?"

"It's kind of obnoxious, are you sure you want me to tell you?" he said.

"You've made it sound like it's a juicy answer, so I'm gonna be annoyed if you *don't* tell me."

"I used to play football, I was pretty good too. I don't usually brag but considering how far in the past all this was I think it's probably okay to brag a little. I was looking at a full sports scholarship, pre-med, I had it all planned out. Then I got injured, bad ACL tear in my left leg put a stop to all of it. It's corny, so try not to roll your eyes, but I had an amazing physiotherapist and… hey, no smirking!"

"They helped you and you wanted to help people the same way, I'm not smirking I'm just— this is how people react to a story like that. You are meeting people at their worst and turning things around for them, I can't think of a better way to make a living." I wanted to add 'it's cute!' to the end of my sentence, but I wasn't sure if that was something an adult man in his forties would want to hear.

"You must have had moments like that when you were nursing," he said.

"I did," I nodded, "I mean you end up basically living at the hospital and even when you're not physically there your brain doesn't switch off. I would get into bed and be thinking about patients, then I'd dream about the ward, and then wake up to a checklist of tasks that I'd started compiling in my sleep."

"Is that why you left?"

"Part of it," I replied, looking up at the entrance to Shaded Wood. We were only a couple of hundred yards away now, but I noticed that Chris had slowed down his walking speed and instinctively I'd done the same. He was prolonging the conversation. I felt my heart race. "I'm gonna stop by and visit dad tomorrow, will you be there?"

"I should be," he nodded. We were barely moving now, the speed at which our feet were carrying us forward was almost comically slow. "I guess I'd better get in there."

"I guess you'd better." He turned to face me and I thought about offering him my phone number, about making arrangements to meet again, about— He reached out a hand to squeeze mine gently, then he continued on to Shaded Wood without me. My fingers tingled as if yearning for him to hold them again, I brought my hand up to my face and pressed it against my cheek.

As I walked the rest of the way to Moody Moon I couldn't help but feel lighter on my feet.

CHAPTER 15

The Moody Moon Hotel was still accessorized with crime scene tape and muddy tire tracks across the front grass. I could almost picture Steve driving the patrol car over the lawn as some petty act of solidarity with Jack. I imagined him laughing as he did it, his stupid little moustache shaking with delight as he gave in to his childish impulses.

Inside, the reception area it was just as I'd left it. No one had been stationed outside to tell me I wasn't allowed in, the tape just told me that it was a crime scene, it didn't even tell me to keep out or that it was restricted access. They must have bought some unofficial police tape from the internet – it was probably Steve's job to sort that out.

I perched myself behind the reception desk and resigned myself to administrative tasks, given that I had over sixty unread emails in my inbox and that I was a relatively slow typist. Disturbingly I'd had a number of customer enquiries for rooms based entirely on the fact that someone was killed here, one or two messages telling me to cleanse my soul and confess, and a few requests for comment from local journalists.

Only one from the Kettle Harbor newspaper; the others worked in neighboring towns. Neighboring in these parts still meant that there were over an hour away.

I deleted the emails from the press, and considered if there was a way of responding to the booking requests without feeling morally bankrupt. Michelle came hurtling through the front doors as if she'd been shot from a cannon, looking hot, angry, and relieved in equal measure.

"What happened to you?" I asked, visibly amused by her appearance. She was not in the mood to see my smiling face, apparently.

"What happened to me? Is that a joke? I'm *this* close to giving you a harsh introduction to some dark magic, that's what. Or maybe I'll just give you some old school punishment and hit you over the head with something!"

I furrowed my brow and tried to work through the list of potential grievances that my older sister could be reacting to. Maybe she'd found out that the scratch down the side of her car was due to one of my unsuccessful parking maneuvers, but that had been months ago. My car was currently rusting in some tow yard across town, surely that was punishment enough. I *really* needed to sort that out.

Maybe she was angry about the fact that I helped myself to a pair of jeans one night when I was at her house because I spilled red wine on the trousers I'd been wearing… I'd helped myself without asking first and then discovered that there was a twenty in the back pocket. I'd kept the twenty. And the jeans.

"You really don't know?" she huffed, her face growing progressively more beetroot by the second.

"You're going to have to narrow it down, Mich."

"Steve. That's what."

"What about Steve?" I asked.

"About an hour ago he showed me photographs of *your* car parked outside O'Malley's on Saturday night. You have no alibi to account for your whereabouts for pretty much the entire evening, but you can be traced to the street where Casey was last seen. Did you not think it would be worth mentioning that you'd gone to the engagement party?"

"I wasn't there!"

"Gemma from the paper gave a statement that she saw a torn up invitation to the engagement party in your trash can. Steve is building a case, Tess. You knew when and where the party was taking place, you ripped up the invite as if you were angry about it, and then you went to the freaking thing!"

"But I didn't. I parked outside on Friday because it was the closest spot to the dry cleaners. Ask Kathleen! She saw me there, I was picking up a dress. By the time I got back to the car it wouldn't start. Hardly a surprise considering the state of it, it's shocking I managed to drive it at all. It's been towed since. I went to the island with Lena, she got called back to work and I stayed there for a while, got frightened half to death by our grandma, then woke up at home."

She held her hands over her face and let out a muffled scream, gravelly and harsh. By the time she moved her arms back down to her sides she had managed to compose herself enough to walk over to the reception desk and lean against it as she spoke, "I've never seen him so motivated to gather evidence. This is literally the most efficient he's ever been and it's because he's determined to get you for this, Tess."

"But I didn't—"

"Your car was there and no one can vouch for you after Lena left you on the island. There aren't cameras outside the bar, so it's not like we can confirm how long the car had been there," she explained.

"You said Steve had photographs…"

"Yeah, some people at the party were taking 'selfies' outside the bar and your car is in the back of the shot. This is what I mean about efficiency, Steve's tracked down the people that were at the bar last night and asked for any pictures they had to see if he can form a timeline of Casey's movements. That's actual police work, how's he even heard of doing something like that?" she huffed.

"What about DNA evidence? Can't you look for fibers on her clothes or something?" I asked.

"She was thrown into a swimming pool, Tess. That messes up a lot of the things we would want to look at."

"So then he only has circumstantial evidence, and you can't get arrested for that, can you?"

"Have you ever read a newspaper? People get put in prison for stuff they didn't do every day in the country. Why do you think the Innocence Project exists? The system is flawed. I've seen people put away with *less* that Steve has on you now," she replied.

I leaned back in the chair and stared up at the ceiling. A scream from outside caused me to lurch forward, panic flooded me and I scrambled to my feet and followed the sound to the back door leading out to the pool area. It wasn't until I was standing at the sunlight bouncing off the rippling water than I realized no one was out here, not even Michelle. It took her a few extra seconds to join me.

"Did you hear that?" I asked. "There was a— I heard something."

"Like what?" she said, looking at me in the same way that she would have if I'd told her I'd spotted an alien ship landing in my back yard.

"A scream, it was… I heard it but—"

"Was it Casey?" she pressed. "Can you… can you *see* her, Tess?"

I looked back at the water, the brightness of the reflected light was almost blinding and I squinted to look for signs of a woman I knew to be dead. Had I lost my mind? I'd seen my grandmother's ghost, sure, but this was something else.

"You have to focus, that's what the book said," Michelle added.

"What book?"

"One of the half dozen on your bedroom floor that you haven't opened yet. Look, Gran *chose* to appear to you, just like she chooses to appear to me and everyone else at our book club. Most ghosts don't really do that. But there are some witches with the sight, and maybe you're one of them. I mean, you were picking up signs of gran's ghost before she managed to break through to you properly, to me that sounds like you're more sensitive to that world…"

"If this is a prank, you've picked a bad day. Is Lena round the corner? Sure, pick on the witch that has no clue what's going on. If this is about the jeans, Mich, then you can have them back. I'll even walk to the ATM right now and get you twenty dollars," I grumbled.

"*You* took that twenty?" she gasped. "Well you can definitely pay me back, but I'm not making stuff up, I swear."

I watched as Michelle held out her hands, palms upwards as if she were holding an invisible book. She closed her eyes and slowly a thick, leather-bound tome materialized. She began to flick through the pages in search of something.

"You can just make stuff appear? Then how on earth did I managed to steal a pair of jeans from you? You could have whipped them right off my body as I was walking around town in them. I'm actually surprised you didn't, because—"

"Got it!" she said, cutting me off. "It says, *'the sight often appears as a white light to those with an untrained eye. Those gifted will be able to focus on the light over time until vision is developed enough to easily communicate with the spiritual plane. Those without this gift will only experience a coldness in the air when in close proximity to a ghost.'* Huh. I don't think I've read this before. There's a cold spot in the bathroom and I always figured the heating was just busted but maybe my house is haunted."

"What do you mean by *focus*?" I screeched, growing increasingly alarmed by the bright light in the pool.

"Where are your glasses?" she asked.

"Glasses? I…" I had been given a prescription for glasses about two years ago, it was supposed to help me with reading but I could get by just fine without them. Okay, I didn't like the look of them. *Fine*, it was actually Jack who didn't like the look of them. He'd said they age me, can you believe it? He'd made me self-conscious enough about having them on my face in public that I'd decided to squint instead.

I'd tried out contact lenses when I'd still been working at the hospital, I'd needed to read patient files and make notes. But then I'd left the hospital and decided that I really didn't like putting things in my eyes, so I'd given up on them entirely. Jacks' words had held such a power over me, I felt embarrassed about how I'd allowed myself to be treated in hindsight.

"Tess, glasses!"

"They're in the drawer of my nightstand," I replied.

Michelle rolled her eyes and tutted at me, "not doing much good there, are they?" Once again she held out her hands and I watched my glasses case materialize onto her palm. She opened them up and handed me the frames which I quickly slipped into place.

So *this* is what the world looks like now. The edges are sharp and defined, colors vivid. "Whoa! Have you ever noticed the—?"

"The pool, look at the pool!" Michelle interrupted.

"Right," I nodded, turning my head. I stared at the light, willing it to take shape. It glowed a little brighter, and then dimmed to reveal a figure. Casey. She was swimming through the pool, beneath the surface. "Casey!" I called out. She stopped in place, using her arms to spin her body around in the water to face me. For a second I admired her breath control to stay submerged for so long, then remembered she probably didn't need to worry about an oxygen supply anymore.

"Tess?!" she replied, "are you talking to me?"

"I sure am," I said, as astonished as she was. Her body lifted up out of the water and floated a few feet in the air, before gliding over to the ground in front of me and dropping to her feet. Michelle had the fingernails of both hands digging into my right forearm, attempts to shake her off were futile.

"Ask her who killed her!" Michelle insisted.

"She can't see me?" Casey asked. I shook my head. "You're the only one that's looked at me since… that whole last day is just such a jumble. I don't remember any of it. I was getting ready, I was curling my hair and then— I just remember being here and looking down at my own body."

"I was kind of hoping you'd be able to point us in the right direction," I sighed. "Sorry, that sounded selfish and obviously I'm sorry that someone, you know, *murdered* you."

"From your tone I'm guessing they haven't caught the person that did it."

"No. The police think I killed you – it's just one offer actually but he seems to be on a mission with this one, so he's not really looking into alternative theories. I *didn't* by the way, just in case that wasn't clear."

"I'll have to take your word for it, because you're the only one that can talk to me," she smiled. "This is kind of messed up, right? I mean, I am just the last person on earth that you want to see or talk to, and now I'm sort of haunting your hotel. I have tried to leave but I think I'm trapped here."

"Isn't it wild that you've been avoiding her for months and now you're the only person who can see her?" Michelle said, almost simultaneously. "I guess you're both going to have to work through your differences because you're stuck with each other!"

"Yeah…" I sighed, agreeing with both of them.

I woke up in my bed without an alarm at seven o'clock sharp after a record breaking twelve hours of sleep. Michelle and I had sat on one of the poolside benches and taken turns reading out sections of the book aloud, which was where we learned that the 'sight' can be exhausting at first before the brain is able to process what the eyes are seeing more easily.

I'd also had to contend with the fact that Michelle couldn't hear Casey, so frequently started talking over her and I had been forced to listen to two conversations at once. As my sister was supposed to be on duty, she couldn't waste her entire afternoon with me at the hotel. She offered me a ride home and I took it, there was no easy way to get out of the awkward conversation with Casey otherwise.

This woman had lured my husband into bed, and my life had imploded. I'd left my job, left my home, and taken over my gran's hotel just to keep my distance from her. But now she was living in my freaking swimming pool. The universe clearly has a dark sense of humor.

I'd gotten home and made a few work calls – mostly to book a cleaner to take care of the muddy police footprints that had been stomped through the reception area, a lot of the folks I called said they wouldn't go near the place if I paid them which was an odd choice of phrase considering that I was obviously offering them money to do that very thing.

A hot bath and a microwave dinner later, I'd climbed into bed with the intention of reading more of the book Michelle had summoned, but when I opened my eyes at seven o'clock sharp I found the book next to me on the pillow – I hadn't read a single page.

I wrapped myself in a fuzzy bathrobe and grabbed my glasses from my nightstand, slipping them onto my face before crossing the room to look at myself in the mirror. There were a million reasons why Jack Stevens should go to hell, and one of them was for making me think these glasses didn't look good. What did I ever see in him?

The windowsill behind me was reflected in the mirror and sitting proudly in the middle of it was the potted plant that Chris had given to me as a gift at my little launch party. I felt my heart flutter at the memory of it, then headed downstairs to make breakfast.

It wasn't until I opened the refrigerator and stared at the empty shelves inside it that I remembered I hadn't been to the grocery store in over a week. I picked up a carton of milk and sniffed at the contents; it was a hazard to human health. I closed the door, tipped the milk away, then began searching the cupboards for *something* to eat. I had teabags, coffee beans, some sort of rice cake thing from when I started my last diet attempt, and a pack of microwavable cauliflower rice from the attempt before.

I closed the cupboard, keeping hold of the handle for a second as I hunched over the counter and considered banging my head against it. It seems a little unfair that I have to earn money to survive in the first place, but around the hours when I'm working I have to find time to spend it on stocking the house with food, cleaning the house after I've prepared said food, and *laundry?* You never see monkeys having to worry about these things. We never should have evolved, huge mistake.

My hands felt warm, and I stood upright to look at the fingers still wrapped around the cupboard handle. They were glowing. I pulled open the door and saw that the shelves were no longer bare, but stocked with all my usual favorites. I turned to the refrigerator and found that inside it was a fresh carton of milk, fresh eggs, cheese, fruits… everything I would have gotten for myself if I'd managed to make it to the store.

I gorged myself in front of the TV, flicking between channels until I found on old episode of Diagnosis Murder that had only just started. I dressed, tamed my hair, and gazed at my reflection for a few moments before deciding that I would take the glasses off, but pack them in my purse incase I needed them later. My self-confidence was a work in progress, and as I was headed to Shaded Wood to visit dad, I figured I would hold off on letting Chris see me in all my bespectacled glory.

I passed the bakery on Barksdale, turned onto Bridge Street and crossed over to be close to the ocean. I passed Whale Watch and spotted Scott waving at me wildly from his boat. "Tess! Come and have a look at this!" he hollered.

"I thought you were taking a few days off," I said, climbing aboard.

"I am! But that doesn't mean I plan on staying away from the water. I came to see how they were getting on with the reupholstering, it looks great! Don't you think?"

"Yeah, it looks brand new in here," I nodded, admiring the newly polka-dot covered seats. "When are you open for business again?"

"Beats me," he shrugged. "We had that high tide on Saturday night a few hours early, I don't know if there was an offshore earthquake or what but we are just waiting for a few days until it all settles down. You can get aftershocks for up to three days after the big one."

I looked over at the building where Lisa was sat at her computer happily typing on dry land. She smiled and waved when she spotted me, and I could swear I saw her wink – but as I didn't have my glasses on I wasn't entirely sure.

"I don't remember seeing the high tide early," I muttered, thinking back to my time on Kettle Island Saturday night. "What time was that?"

"The land bridge is always submerged a few hours before high tide, so people could have gone over to the island and gotten back up until eleven o'clock according to the charts. I looked out around eight and the whole thing was under water, I'm surprised I didn't get called out to rescue tourists that got trapped out there, we're still waiting on the emergency phone line to get fitted. We've just been keeping an eye on folks crossing and I sometimes do a lap of the island in case anyone is waiting on the shore for a pick up."

"Yeah, I heard about people getting stuck out there overnight..." I said. What time had it been when I passed out on the island? Gran had shown up and scared me half to death, then I'd woken up at home the next morning. Had my use of magic affected the tide? "Anyway, I should get going. I've got a date with an old man that still isn't speaking."

"I heard he's started taking steps again, though. I think Michelle mentioned it to Lisa. Do you think you'd be getting him out of Shaded Wood when he's back on his feet?"

"One thing at a time, Scott, jeez," I laughed. Dad had gone there for the kind of help and support I wasn't able to provide while also holding down a full time job. If he was more self-sufficient then he probably could leave that place, but I hadn't even thought about it yet. "I'll cross that bridge when I come to it."

"I supposed he'd be moving in with either you or your sister, right?" he asked.

"Scott—"

"Yeah, yeah. One thing at a time," he chuckled. "I personally would rather boil my own head that have my dad come and live with me, but that's because he's a total nightmare. He puts the TV on full volume and then just falls asleep, the driveway outside is vibrating with the soundwaves and he's snoring away in the armchair like he can't hear a thing. Anyway, I'll let you get going. Have you made a plan for tomorrow?"

"What's tomorrow?"

"The funeral. I thought you would have heard."

"*Casey's* funeral? How did they arrange that so fast?!" I exclaimed.

"In Ireland they have the funeral two or three days after death," he added.

"Yeah, but we're not in Ireland, are we?" I said, rubbing at my temples. If I stay away I look guilty, if I show up I look brazen. What was the social etiquette on attending the funeral of a woman you are accused of strangling? Was there a 'good house-keeping' guide for that? Jack wouldn't be above causing a scene, either. I could imagine him yelling at me across the graveyard. "I'll have to think about it, the situation is a little *delicate* at the moment, so—"

"Steve on your back? He was sniffing round here yesterday trying to dig up dirt on you."

"He was?" I grimaced.

"He's trying to poke holes in your story about being on the island when Casey was killed. He wanted to know if we'd seen you walking over there given that we're sort of unofficially tracking folk in case they get stuck out there," he explained.

"And?"

"I said I had nothing to say to him and sent him packing. I'm not playing any part in him coming after you for this," Scott said, proudly. I was lucky to have friends in the right places. I thanked Scott for his support, gave another wave to Lisa, then hurried off towards the care home.

* * *

THE DAY ROOM was the usual, sedate atmosphere with the exception of two older women playing snap and giggling as they somewhat slowly tried to race their hands onto matching pairs of cards. Louise rose to her feet when she saw me enter and walked out from behind the nurses station.

"He's gone swimming!" she announced. "Chris offered to take him to the therapy pool and they've been out for the last half hour. I don't know when he's planning on bringing him back but he's got another appointment soon so he shouldn't be long."

"Swimming, huh?"

"Mmhmm. Helping to rebuild the strength in his legs without

putting too much strain on 'em. That man of yours is taking good care of your dad, don't you worry," she winked.

"Oh, he isn't my— it's not really like that, I just—"

"I know more about what goes on around here than I let on," she smiled. "I think one of my *special* skills is picking up on hushed conversations. It's either a witch thing or I'm so nosey that my hearing improved! Hard to tell."

"Are you going to the funeral tomorrow?" I asked.

"Yeah. A few of the residents have said they wanna go, too. I figure they just want a day out, even if it is to a graveyard. I'm driving the minivan and a few of the people I'm taking have a habit of 'backseat driving', so pray for me. You going?"

"I don't know yet, I only just heard it was happening. It just seems like a rush, or am I crazy? When have you ever known someone have a funeral so fast? She was young, so it's not as if anyone anticipated that they'd need to be arranging a funeral soon," I said.

"Look, I hate gossiping…" she said, leaning closer to me to no doubt engage in some top-tier rumor spreading, "but I hear that she had life insurance."

"What? She was twenty-nine!"

"Yeah, but the younger you are when you start the cheaper it is, that's how they get'ya, those companies hook you in with lower rates so you think you're getting yourself covered for a steal. What else would be motivating Jack to get the funeral taken care of so quickly? I think there's money to be had, and he's wrapping up this whole sorry mess as fast as he can."

Well there goes another bullet point in the column under Jacks name on my mental suspect list. I turned to look through the window at the back lawn and noticed a faint light at the far end of the grass. Perhaps another opportunity to put my newfound sight to the test. "Would I be alright walking around out back until my dad shows up?"

"Do your thing. I used to walk laps around that lawn on my lunch breaks every day but now my hip aches when it's cold out and I think I've gotten some kind of hay fever or something because being outdoors sets me off sneezing. Kathleen said she had something that would help with the allergies but I'm pretty sure it was just a shot of whisky… that woman needs to get herself some help because the drinking is just the start, you watch…" Louise trailed off as she wandered back behind the nurse's station.

I accidentally made eye contact with the angry grandmother of Bobby – Casey's stalker. She grunted in my direction and then beckoned me to her with a bony finger. If I had to guess I'd say she'd used that finger for a lot of wagging in her time, barking orders at small children while threatening to tell the true story about the big man in red at the North Pole.

"Yes?" I said. My tone was one of a woman in her forties who did not appreciate being summoned like a naughty dog.

"He ain't here," she replied.

"Who? My dad? I know."

"Not your father, why would I give a stuff about your father?"

"Don't get a lot of visitors, do you? I can't imagine why…" I huffed.

"Bobby ain't here. If you've come to make accusations about my grandson then think again, missy, because he's turned things around."

"Oh?"

"You think I'm stupid don't ya? I know you're type. Your one of those that talks louder to old people 'cause you think we're all deaf, you think my brains have melted out of both ears. I'm smart as a whip, don't you dare forget it!" she snapped.

"I have barely said a word to you, how are you getting all that from what I've said?"

"Your sister is in the police. They're a crooked bunch, out to get my Bobby when he's only ever trying his best. You think just because he's got priors that he's the one that hurt Casey, he loved that girl! He was too good for her, though. She couldn't see just how special he is and it broke his heart! Girls always break his heart, he's a sensitive soul. You women are all the same!" As I anticipated, she punctuated her rant with a finger wag that could bring an army general to his knees.

"You women? Are you not included in that group? And what do you mean he has priors?"

"Don't play dumb with me. I know your game, you're in with the police – feeding them information about Bobby and what you've seen here, waiting for him to be dragged off to court again. They dragged his name through the mud once, so it doesn't surprise me they'd try it again!"

"Time for your meds, Iris," Louise interrupted, turning to me and mouthing *'sorry about her'.*

Iris continued to snarl at me as I backed away and headed for the door to the back yard. Obviously I then pulled my cell phone out of my pocket and dialed my sister's number.

CHAPTER 17

"Tess, I'm not involved in this case, you know why," Michelle replied.

"Yeah, but I'm asking you about something else."

"Look, the officers involved have to follow the evidence related to *this* case. It wouldn't matter if we had some sort of serial strangler running around town, you can't just assume that's it is the person that's done something similar without any evidence to connect them to the crime."

"Is this your roundabout way of telling me that Bobby has stran-gled people before?" I asked.

"Google it," she replied. "All I can say to you is that Bobby had an alibi, Steve told me that he's spoken to him and he's been cleared."

"But Steve is a moron with idiot jelly where his brain should be!"

"I agree, but Steve said the alibi checks out. Have you spoken with Charlotte again since Sunday?" she asked. I'd almost forgotten about Charlotte.

"No, I haven't. Is *she* going to tell me what horrific crimes Bobby has committed in the past?"

"Just give her a call later, Steve was here late last night and he's never worked past his scheduled hours in all the years he's worked here. He's like a dog with a bone on this one. Speak to Charlotte, make sure she knows what's going on."

Before I had a chance to respond I could hear the dial tone. She'd hung up. During the conversation I'd made it a quarter of the way around the lawn at the back of Shaded Wood and was now within a hundred feet of the bright light I'd noticed from the day room.

"Well! I'm just hoping that whoever you are you have more time to talk to me that my own sister does. You know you'd think that me being prime suspect in a murder investigation and going through some sort of magical menopausal transformation would be enough to justify being the center of attention for at least a week," I huffed, digging through my purse for my glasses. "*Oh Tess, a guy a work with is coming for you with laser focus and there's nothing I can do about it! Good luck with that!*', I would have been such a good only child – you have no idea."

I put the glasses on, and the ghost of an older gentlemen came into focus in front of me, his mouth hung open as if astonished.

"Hello, my name is Theresa and apparently I have some sort of special ghost sight that means I can—"

"Ma'am, I have been circling the lawn at the back of this facility for almost fifteen years. I have not had someone look me in the eye since I died out here and I'll be dammed if the first conversation I have since my passing is with a woman in the middle of a breakdown. I'm not a therapist! Take your problems to someone else!"

He turned to face in the opposite direction and floated away at a speed akin to sprinting, looking back over his shoulder every few seconds to check I wasn't following him.

"Oh good! I've scared away a ghost, that's just excellent," I muttered, half-laughing.

"So you can see him?"

I turned to see Lionel in his birthday suit standing on the grass beside me. It didn't seem to register as unusual anymore, which was a problem. "*You* can see him?" I asked.

"Not well, but yes. My wife was like you, she had the sight," he replied. "Our daughter has powers, but she didn't inherit that particular gift."

"Oh." It caught me off guard. What was the protocol for talking about magic with people outside of the book club? "I didn't realize."

"I don't blame you. I've made a name for myself around here as the naked guy, no one takes me seriously. Understandable really. Mind if I join you?" he asked, gesturing ahead of us as if we were about to take a Jane Austen-style walk on the grounds. Just me in a pair of ugly glasses and a man older than my father wearing not a single stitch of clothing or shoes. A normal Tuesday.

"Why not?" I said. This week can't get any weirder, no point trying to steer away from the unusual now. "So you said you can't see the ghosts well? How do they appear to you?"

"Like whisps of smoke, as if someone just blew out a candle. I can sometimes hear their voices, but my hearing isn't the best anymore. Have you seen Casey's ghost by any chance?"

"Yes, I did actually. She doesn't remember what happened to her though, I *did* ask. Back to the drawing board with that one," I replied. I was now holding my hands in front of my waist, interlacing my fingers as if I were on a stroll with Mr. Darcy. I couldn't wait to recount this to Lena at some point. I bet dad would find this whole thing pretty funny too.

"Such a shame. She had her whole life ahead of her, and I heard she was a potential! You can never have too many of those in this town!"

"How do you know so much about all this?" I asked.

"My wife kept me in the loop, I'm still waiting on her ghost to show up actually. I think she'll find this whole 'nudist' act quite amusing," he grinned. "My childhood sweetheart, a beauty by anyone's standards and what a laugh! It was like music; I'd do anything to hear it again – even walk around without clothes just in case she's watching!" he chuckled.

"I can keep a look out for you," I offered with a shrug.

"Would you? Oh I appreciate that. You'll know her when you see her, she's got a wicked sense of humor. Her name is Mary-Jo, a real rose among thorns. You know I think I fell for her the moment we met." He was smiling from ear to ear at the memory of it, "she reached out a hand to introduce herself and there was an electricity when we touched. For the longest time we were just in the same social circles and I would do anything and everything to try and talk to her. I heard a rumor that one of the other guys we knew was hoping to ask her out and it broke my heart."

"So what happened?"

"I took a chance," he replied proudly. "I told her that I was in love in a way that I couldn't shake loose or try to forget about, that the thought of her being with someone else made my chest ache. You know, she heard me out and she stood there without saying a word for what felt like eternity. The knot in my stomach tightened with each passing second that I waited for her to say *anything*. Just when I looked down at my shoes she reached out her hand just like she had the first time, she grabbed hold of mine and... well she didn't let go until two years ago, let's put it that way!"

"Then I'll *definitely* keep an eye out for her," I smiled.

"That's why I always say you should take a leap of faith with matters of the heart. If you have a connection with a person then throw yourself into it! I know you're marriage didn't work out, but the next one might!"

"You should work in the marketing department of a dating website," I laughed.

"Liam told me something similar! I think I'd come up with the line, *'this one might be THE one',* and he told me that I should send that line to a company that makes apps for swiping. I didn't know what he meant but he told me—"

"Liam?" I interrupted.

"Yes, he hasn't been in for a few days which... after what that poor boy went through."

I stopped walking and turned to face him, briefly forgetting that he was naked top to toe. "What do you mean?"

"I know what heartache looks like, I saw it on his face daily over the last year, then a few months ago I started to figure out what was going on. He was in love with Casey, had been since they were teenagers—" I wanted to point out that *teenagers* for them was basically five minutes ago, but it was unnecessarily catty so I decided to keep my mouth closed, "— I think the engagement sent him over the edge actually. I said to him that he was running out of time if he wanted to get the girl. Last I heard he was planning to tell her how he felt, obviously I gave a very motivational speech which prompted him to—"

"Whoa, back up!" I said. "He came to the hotel on Friday night— he was by the pool with my dad. When was he planning on declaring his feeling for Casey? When did you talk to him?"

"It will have been on Friday afternoon; I think your sister showed up to take your father up the road to your party and I'd just about finished telling him. He'd had to escort me to my room to put clothes on before visiting hours started, I remember that much, and I said to him that he should say something before the wedding at the very least. What if she felt the same way? His hesitancy could be depriving them both of *the* relationship that they are supposed to be in!"

"Oh jeez," I sighed. He gave a desperate man a time limit, never a good idea. If I was the 'leaping to conclusions' type – which I was – then I'd say that Liam *did* tell Casey how he felt and it wasn't reciprocal. Was he the man she was arguing with outside O'Malley's? Chris said Casey had been driving Liam around since his car broke down, taking him to and from work. What if she drove him to Shaded Wood *from* the engagement party and then he snapped and killed her? The hotel is right by here, he already knew there was a pool because he'd been standing next to it the night before.

"Lionel!" Louise screeched from the back door of the day room. "I know you ain't out here with a visitor right now! Get yourself dressed before I come out there and—"

"That's my cue to leave!" Lionel laughed, a wild glint in his eye. He started sprinting away at an impressive speed and I looked back to see Louise tracking his movements while shaking her head.

I started to slowly walk back in her direction, trying to detangle the mess that Lionel had just unloaded onto me. Liam knew about the bruises on Casey, he probably figured they were Jack's doing just like I had. What would you do if the woman you were in love with was about to marry someone like that? Someone that would hurt her, that cheated on his first wife and would quite likely do it again? As far as I was aware, Jack had only had *one* affair, but he wasn't getting any bonus points for going on to propose to the girl.

Liam could have confessed his feelings and been rejected. Rejected so that she could go on to marry a man that Liam knew was bad for her. That would hurt. His ego wounded; he could have lashed out.

"What on earth were the two of you talking about?" Louise asked, eyeing me suspiciously.

"His wife was a witch; did you know that?"

"MJ? Yeah, she was friends with your grandmother but never fancied being part of our little book club. I think she had more *conservative* tastes and one time Kathleen suggested a 'novel' – and I use the word loosely – that involved one woman and four men and all five of them would—"

"That's enough. I don't need to know about that book, because you are implying that MJ didn't stick around because that book got selected for book club which meant both my sister and my grandmother read it."

"I think your grandma could re-write that thing from memory. You should have heard the review she gave it; you'd think it was a Ray Bradbury the way she went on," Louise laughed, reveling in my discomfort. "Your dad's back, by the way. Chris said the swimming went really well. Still ain't talking though…"

"I know. I should get Gran to show up in his room and start talking about this spicy book she loves so much, I bet he'd start talking then just to tell her to get the hell out!" I laughed.

I stepped into the day room and spotted dad in his wheelchair, a smile on his face when he caught sight of me. I was about to search the room for Chris, but dad waved his hand to get my attention back, thumbed over his shoulder, made his fingers and thumb on his right hand clap together over and over in the way people do when they are miming someone talking too much, then pointed at me. He had been gesturing to Chris who was behind him at the reception desk.

Chris had been talking about me.

I sat on an armchair beside my dad and he held up both hands balled into fists, releasing one finger at a time until he was holding up nine, then held up the tenth and shrugged with raised brows. *How many ghost sightings are you up to now?*

It wasn't official sign language, but it worked for us.

"Michelle took me to her little book club, I saw Gran there," I said. He nodded, knowingly. I checked that no one else in the room was close enough to overhear before continuing, "I've only been to one of them so far and Kathleen gave me enough wine to take down an elephant. It's honestly a miracle that I pulled through. Oh, and apparently Gran was into some *really* interesting books. I'm talking romance with a 'triple-X' warning on the front."

He pulled his face into a grimace and nodded again, this was to say *'yeah, I knew that, and I wish I didn't.'*

"Did you know that Liam was in love with Casey?" I asked. Dad nodded. "Oh. See this is why you need to start talking to me again because I just spent the past few minutes thinking I was pulling a Sherlock Holmes or something. You already knew, huh? I suppose you already knew Casey's car was parked out the back too, huh?"

He nodded again, pointed at his eyes, then out to the parking lot. *He'd seen her.*

"She was here on Saturday night? You saw her here?" I asked. He nodded again. "Was she with Liam?" Another nod.

CHAPTER 18

ednesday morning rolled around and I was happily sitting at my kitchen table minding my own business when my sister barged into the house. She was talking as if in the middle of a conversation and I figured she was on the phone, but when she made her way to where I was I could see that she was talking to my grandmother.

"But if we don't show up then people could die! I'm a police officer, it's not weird if I go!" she continued.

"And I suggested that keeping your distance would be more appropriate given the circumstances. Please keep the hyperbolic language to a minimum, Michelle, because I do not think there is any risk to the lives of the attendees today. It is of course a daytime event, which you may recall is a powerful deterrent for those types."

"*Those types.* They're not a group of bikers, Gran, and need I remind you that vampires don't care about sunlight anymore?" Michelle continued. I took another bite of my bagel and turned the page of the newspaper I was reading. They'd let me know when they wanted me to contribute to whatever this was.

"I was not under the impression that Kathleen had provided us with a historically accurate account of modern vampire life," Gran added sarcastically. "Are you anticipating a few beautiful young men showing up at the funeral with glittering skin and prominent abdominal muscles?"

"I'm not saying it's like Twilight, I'm saying that those patients showing up at the hospital weren't all attacked at night. I just think that a group gathering in the cemetery is like an all you can eat buffet but if we *all* show up, that means you too, Tess—" Michelle said, dragging me into it "— then they wouldn't dare."

"Hold on," I said, reluctantly lowering my bagel, adjusting my bath robe and staring at the two of them. "You think I'm going to Casey's funeral to protect the town from a vampire attack? Have you lost your mind?"

"Kathleen has been raving about vampires for quite some time, Theresa. It does not surprise me that she has convinced another witch that this is a serious problem," Gran said.

"There have been attacks already, I didn't make those up. Lena saw the patients in the hospital, I took statements from them about what happened. This is real, Gran," Michelle exclaimed.

"Has anyone died?" she asked. Michelle shook her head. "Then what is the harm?"

"You think that we should let them carry on drinking blood from people at will because they're only having a little snack? Unbelievable," Michelle grumbled, pulling out a chair at the table and reaching over to steal what was left of my bagel.

"I was planning on staying home and cleaning the house," I said.

"It certainly needs it," Gran added.

"I've got books about magic that are upstairs just gathering more dust, I have to sort a load of laundry out because the creases are just out of control, and— oh, I called you yesterday a few times Michelle. I think Liam strangled Casey, I went over to the station to tell you about it and put in a statement, but I spotted Steve behind reception and managed to shuffle back outside before he noticed me. I figured he wouldn't hear me out, so my best bet—"

"Liam?" Michelle interrupted.

"Yeah, he works at Shaded Wood. He was in love with her, got goaded into announcing it by a naked old man, and then I reckon it didn't go the way he hoped. Dad said he spotted the two of them outside the care home on Saturday, she'd been driving him to work recently and maybe he asked her to take her from the engagement party and then lashed out."

"Interesting," she hummed.

"Interesting, *how?* Interesting as in 'oh good one, Sis, I'll get this guy arrested right away', or interesting like 'we already cleared him', or—"

"No, I don't think he's been taken off the list. Get me another bagel and I'll fill you in," she said, eyeing up the pack that I'd left out on the counter. My nostrils flared only slightly as I stood up to complete the task I'd been blackmailed into, but Michelle started talking as I sliced and toasted. "I have read through a few witness statements from the engagement party crowd, when Steve wasn't looking obviously."

"And?"

"Jack had sunk three whiskeys within forty minutes of arriving, offering to buy a round for everyone and making toasts about his bride-to-be. He was clearly drunk, and no one saw Casey drinking anything alcoholic – she was the designated driver apparently. You know what he's like after a drink, he gets loud. Loud is usually the stage before aggressive, remember when he yelled at Christmas because I said he'd had enough to drink?"

"I do," I sighed. I really should have left him a long, long time ago. It had been one of those gatherings where someone completely embarrasses themselves – Jack in this case – and everyone else stands around awkwardly looking at anything in the room besides the spectacle in the center of it. I'd pulled his arm to get him to turn around, gave him *the stare* (a thing that all married couples establish subconsciously) and he knew he'd crossed a line.

He gave Michelle a half-hearted apology then claimed he had to go into the hospital early the following day to review patient notes and so the two of us left early and went home. I'd been mortified and left him to nurse a hangover alone as penance. I felt lucky that my family could still love me even when I wasn't loving myself properly.

"Anyway, Jack was making an ass of himself and then at some point he left. No one saw him for about an hour and a half, then he was back again. At some point during all this, Casey left too. Like I said, only Jack came back," Michelle continued.

"Does Jack have an alibi for that time?" I asked.

"He isn't currently aware that we know he left," Michelle replied. "He told Steve he was there the entire night, only left at closing and then went home. Steve asked him where he thought Casey had gotten to and he said he figured she was at work."

"I see," I said, flinching as the toaster fired sliced bagels upward. I started spreading cream cheese across them and thinking about the theory that Jack had strangled someone to death. Was it selfish to be thinking about how that would affect *me?* I would have divorced a murderer, that would be a stain on my name as much as it was a stain on his – almost. Obviously he would get jail time and all I would get would be people trying to bring it up in conversations around town.

"Steve *has* to know that his buddy is on the hook for this," Michelle said.

"If you are planning to attend the funeral then you might want to start getting ready, Theresa, because you have crumbs in your cleavage and you need to run a comb through that hair before you are fit for public consumption," Gran announced.

"Tess, Kathleen is confident that vampires might zone in on the graveyard with all these people today. They put the time and date in the paper, they are expecting a big turnout and a candle procession afterwards. It's standard when someone young dies, especially when justice is yet to be served. It riles up the community and then they show up in droves to the funeral and… Kathleen will be there. So will Louise and me. She's been hounding Lisa with phone calls, too."

"Lena?" I said. As if she'd heard her own name, Lena came through the front door and announced her arrival.

"It's only me, Tess. Nightmare at the hospital, two consultants said they planned to go to Casey's funeral because they'd worked with her and it was such a loss and blah blah blah. Both of them have *just* got back from separate golf trips – although if you ask me there's a little more action happening between the sheets than on the green! Anyway, they are barely ever on the ward as it is and then they've— Oh hi, Michelle. Linda," Lena said, acknowledging my sister and grandmother's presence in the room.

"So you're short staffed?" I said, prompting her to keep talking.

"Oh yeah, so they decided yesterday they're going to this thing and then we realize that because there are also nurses going too that we were going to be down a few people. Anyway, long story short, I had to cover someone's overnight shift because *they* were covering the day shift. Are there any bagels left?" she asked.

"Sure, help yourself," I shrugged, walking away from the counter in case I got tricked into making another person's breakfast for the second time today. "You're going to the funeral then?" It was a joke considering that Lena was dressed in a pair of black trousers, black heels, and a black blouse. Not her usual, cheery wardrobe.

"Kathleen said we had to. I was all for going straight to my bed and sleeping until dusk, but apparently we are the last line of defense between the human population of Kettle Harbor and the vampire horde invading our shores. She can be quite the William Wallace when she wants to be. Are you *not* going, Tess?"

"I thought I was too old to give in to peer pressure," I huffed. "Could I stay back? I don't want Jack to see me because—"

"Because he thinks you killed Casey?" Lena guessed.

"That's *one* of the reasons, yes. Are you going to make sure that Steve probes into the missing hour and a half of his Saturday night, Michelle?" I asked.

"If he doesn't, then I will. I think trying to see if Steve is capable of doing the right thing hasn't worked out so well, so I'm just going to have to take over and let the public opinion about it fall where it may. I'm sure the newspapers will have a freaking picnic when they find out the police station is dancing on a thin ethical line. They've rarely got anything interesting to write about," Michelle replied.

I leaned against the kitchen counter and looked at the three of them. This past week had been the most I'd seen any of them in a long time – obviously my grandma had died so she could be forgiven for not visiting frequently over the last couple of months. Lena and Michelle, though? I didn't ever imagine them really being in the same room as each other, but they'd been having secret 'book club' meetings and hanging out without me.

"Come on, Tess. It won't be that bad. I know she ruined your marriage, stole your man and your house, I know all of that. But up until that point, you two got on alright," Michelle said, a half-smile as if she couldn't even convince herself that it was a good idea for me to go with them. "If we see a vampire then we can all team up and blast them back to hell, or wherever it is vampires come from."

"I once heard that it was a mutated, blood-borne disease that had been around for centuries. It came over to the Americas back when—" Gran began, but quickly stopped when she saw the looks on our faces. We didn't want a history lesson. "I was just going to say that it was the fault of the English, but please continue."

"If Jack starts yelling any accusations then I can kick him in his favorite place," Lena smiled. "I'd finally get to check that off my bucket list."

"There's a line for kicking Jack Steven's in the crotch, Lena, and I'm at the front," Michelle added.

"I appreciate the support, I think."

"Once we've made sure that everyone gets out of this funeral alive —" Michelle said, raising a finger to anticipate what Lena was about to jump in with, "not Casey, obviously, but everyone else. Once we've gotten away from the graveyard then we can look into grilling Jack over his whereabouts on Saturday."

"We should get Kathleen to ask him," Lena suggested.

"I'm with the police, it should be me."

"Yes, but who is more intimidating? You or Kathleen? I heard a rumor that she was a prison guard before she got that dry cleaners. I heard that's where she learned how to make wine like that," Lena said.

"You are going to be late," Gran announced, pointing up to the clock. "Try to be on your best behavior, the funeral of a potential is a somber event and as kicking a man between the legs would not be in keeping with the tone. Besides, the line of people interested in doing that would actually start behind *me*, Michelle."

CHAPTER 19

ichelle had offered us a ride in her patrol car, but I figured that it wouldn't look right stepping out of a police vehicle when I already have the 'suspected murderer' target on my back. We had opted for a cab instead.

After a quick round of rock, paper, scissors – which I think was rigged, by the way, as the two woman I was playing with had witch-craft skills far beyond my own – it was decided that *I* would be ringing Kathleen to confirm the details of her vampire fighting 'plan'.

Kathleen answered in a whisper which immediately caused the hairs on my neck to stand up. She informed me that she was hiding in the shrubbery on the outskirts of the graveyard and had been there overnight, that she was in full camouflage gear and that she had a shotgun that she'd loaded up with wood somehow. I could have asked for more details, but I thought it was best to keep the conversation brief.

She wanted to know what weapons we were bringing, if we would be passing a grocery store on the way, and if any of us were packing face powder that could adequately cover a sweaty face. This was incase she deemed the place safe enough that she could leave the shrubbery and join the mourners grave-side.

Did she want a change of clothes? No. Did she intend to leave her shotgun somewhere hidden? No. She planned to walk out of a hedge dressed like she was a member of some elder-militia and home that a thin layer of the half-empty Laura Mercier translucent loose setting powder I had in my purse would be enough to make her look normal.

We piled into the cab that Michelle had ordered for us, and Lena gave the driver instructions to take us to the graveyard via Walgreens – although 'via' implies it was a stop along the route and not a total detour through town.

"Nice day for it," the driver said, jerking his head up towards the sky.

"For a funeral?" I asked.

"Oh, you headed up there for a service?"

"...Yeah," Michelle replied, looking at her own outfit then at the Lena and I, all three of us in black. Do people often get dressed like this and head to a graveyard in a group for fun?

He pulled over outside Walgreens and Lena hopped out; following Kathleen's orders to bring bottled water and a container of salt. Michelle and I waited in the idling cab as the driver continued to talk to us.

"Did you know them well?" he asked.

"Who?" Michelle said. "Oh the person that died? Er... *yes*."

My sister has the worst poker face of anyone I've ever seen. It amazes me that she managed to keep her witchcraft secret from me for so many years because I can usually read her like an open book. I brushed a speck of lint of my left knee and realized that the trousers were not the linen ones I thought I'd grabbed.

I'd tried on a pair of smart, black trousers in the store and when I'd done a three-sixty spin in the changing room I'd been impressed by how they looked from behind – they made my butt look good. Given how rare it is for me to try on clothes and like what I see in the mirror, I'd grabbed a couple of pairs of these trousers from the rack and taken them to the counter.

They made my legs look slimmer, obscured some of the unwanted curves I carried around my middle, and most importantly, pockets.

Real pockets. Not the fake pockets that are sewn up across the top, not the little baby pockets that can barely fit a nickel inside them, but pockets deep enough for a cell phone and a set of car keys.

In my haste I didn't seem to notice that one of the pairs I'd grabbed from the rack was a *slightly* different shade of black. Someone had tried something on, been unhappy with the fit, and put it back in the wrong place, leading me to own two pairs of beautifully thin, comfortable, breathable, pocket-equipped linen trousers... and one pair of polyester. A sweaty person's fiercest enemy. I'd missed the returns window, so now I was stuck with them. I could obviously donate them, or throw them away, but I'd clearly forgotten to do that.

Would now be a terrible time for my hormones to raise my body temperature to a thousand degrees? Yes.

"Can you turn on the AC?" I asked.

"It's busted," the driver replied. "I'm on a waiting list to get it fixed because these things come in threes, don't they?! My AC went, one of the other drivers had to get his exhaust replaced because one of the brackets came loose and it was dragging along the—"

Michelle noticed the glisten developing on my forehead and placed a reassuring hand on my leg, "are those polyester, Tess? What were you thinking?" Before I could answer she lifted her other hand and wiggled a few fingers in the direction of the dashboard, prompting the air conditioning to burst to life and almost immediately cool down the inside of the car. My hero.

"Oh, would you look at that?!" the driver said, half laughing as he thumped a fist down on the dash, "sometimes you've just gotta give it time. Cars can be temperamental, just like women! Ha!"

If it wasn't for the fact that the AC was the only reason I wasn't currently pouring with sweat then I would happily get out of this car right now and walk the rest of the way. Even in these polyester pants.

Lena ran back towards the car with a bag in her arms and hurried back inside, visibly relieved to find the that the air was chilled. "They had a discount on these Junior Mints!" she announced, pulling them out of the bag. "I got enough for everyone!"

Clearly there were two heroes in this car.

She handed us a pack each and we tore into them as the driver pulled away from the curb, and we giddily tore into them. "Here," Michelle said, grabbing the box in my hands and winking at me. I felt the cardboard get cold. "Frozen ones are best."

"Could I grab one of those?" the driver asked.

"Yes, sure," Michelle said, leaning forward ever so slightly, then saying, "just kidding. I meant no. Women are temperamental, remember?" She grinned and popped a few frozen mints into her mouth as the scenery outside raced past the window.

"Oh I was only joking," he laughed. "But you sure do like changing your minds, you know, as a species."

"We're from the same species," Michelle replied, "somehow."

"You know my nephew was engaged to a lovely girl, beautiful thing she was—" as he spoke the three of us mimed vomiting at the use of the word 'thing' – "smart too, or so we thought! My nephew had a bit of trouble at his job and then all of sudden he's out of work. Do you think she stuck around? For better or worse? Ha! Turns out she had been sneaking around with someone else, and then look how that turned out!"

He looked at us in the rear-view mirror, chewing on our frozen mints and shrugging at him in response. "How did it turn out?" Lena offered, concerned that if he didn't look back at the road soon we might veer off into the side of a building.

"Well I'm about to take you to her funeral, I reckon!" he scoffed.

"I'm sorry, *what*!?" I gasped.

"Yeah, well we talked about going and decided against it. People always romanticize the dead but I think you shouldn't automatically get let off the hook. She broke his heart, really messed him up, and I don't think standing around the grave pretending that we were close to her at the end helps anyone," he continued.

"Your nephew was engaged to Casey Quinn?" Michelle repeated.

"Yeah!"

"And what is your nephew's name?" I asked.

"Robert Miller, that's what it says on his birth certificate! Well, it actually says Robert Tag Miller because my sister married an Irishman and they had a thing for old names which—"

"Bobby?!" I said, sitting forward forcefully enough that my seatbelt resisted and tried to pull me back.

"Yeah, do you know him?" he said, pulling into the entrance of the graveyard and coming to a stop. Michelle paid him and we started to file out, not paying a great deal of attention to the driver who was still trying to talk to us as Lena closed the door.

"Okay, well that's a problem," I huffed, pinching the bridge of my nose.

"What? Did you leave something in the car?" Lena asked.

"No! Look, Bobby is a guy that's been stalking her at work, she'd complained, she'd had Louise ban him from the building. I didn't know that they'd been in a relationship with each other at any point. That changes things, the fact that she cheated on him *also* changes things," I explained.

"Bobby has an alibi," Michelle added.

"Yeah according to *Steve*, which quite frankly means nothing."

"So who exactly do you think killed Casey then? I thought you were onto Jack for it because he'd been arguing, and the bruises…" Lena said.

"You were just outlining your Liam theory to me in your kitchen an hour ago," Michelle sighed, I quickly realized that the sigh wasn't aimed at me, but rather aimed at Kathleen who had just stunt rolled behind a tree a hundred feet to our left. It was so silent out here that the sound of her body colliding with the ground, followed by her grunts as she tried to roll and then stand up again, drew our attention. "Kat? Are you okay?"

"Did you bring supplies?" she yelled.

"Sure did!" Lena lifted up the bag from Walgreens and shook it. Kathleen then dropped to a crouch and peered around the tree trunk, looked left and right, then ran in a hunched over position as if evading enemy fire in the trenches. As the owner of the dry cleaners I'd always thought she was reasonably normal, but now that the curtain had been lifted on witchcraft it seemed that she felt more comfortable being her unusual self in front of me.

"I've cleared the perimeter, so far so good," Kathleen said, grabbing the bag from Lena and pulling out *another* box of Junior Mints, tearing off the corner and tipping a dozen of them into her mouth.

I checked my watch; the crowd would be graveside by now. I watched as Kathleen continued to consume Junior Mints at an alarming pace, and wondered if she was really anticipating needing to fight a vampire army this morning, or just wanted an excuse to run around with a weapon. She threw each of us a bottle of water, then another. How many did we need? Was she expecting us to camp out here? I tucked them into my bag which instantly became uncomfortably heavy.

Once she'd finished her snack we started to walk along the path towards the newer graves. The breeze outside was welcome, even though the hot flush was over the polyester was making my legs feel like they were toasting.

"My cleavage is like a log flume for ants right now," Kathleen remarked as she crouched down and dropped the Walgreens bag on the ground. "Right, everyone load up."

I winced, thinking she was about to hand us all guns. Lena and Michelle held out cupped hands and stood still as Kathleen tipped salt into them. "Tess," Michelle prompted, nudging me with her elbow. My sister was now trying to put the salt into her pockets, as was Lena.

"Can you just tip it directly into my pocket from the container? You'd waste less," I said. There was a collective mumble as the three of them realized that it would have been sensible to do that from the beginning. I popped a hip towards Kathleen and held open the pocket of my trousers. "I've gotta ask, why are we doing this?"

"Salt can protect you," Kathleen replied.

"From vampires?"

"No, from… well from everything else," she said. "You can use it to make salt circles around yourself if things get wild. If you stand in the middle it can also enhance your power, so it's best to keep salt on you if you're headed out into battle."

"You are utterly ridiculous," my grandmother added, appearing in a whisp of white smoke with one eyebrow already raised in Kathleen's direction. "This is not a battlefield; it is a graveyard. Salt will not provide a great deal of assistance if you are dealing with a blood thirsty vampire, will it?"

"There could be *other* creatures lurking around out here," Kathleen muttered.

"Why would you be wearing camouflage if you are hunting vampires, anyway? They can detect your scent!" Gran added.

I looked towards the crowd that were just now visible in the distance, all in black and with their heads bowed as if in collective prayer. Even from this distance I was able to make out Officer Steve with his atrocious facial hair. "Can we focus?" I huffed.

"On what, Theresa?" Gran said.

"That." I pointed over at the mass of people, more specifically at the figure standing behind a tree looking on. Someone was watching them. I grabbed my glasses and slipped them onto my face. The details were still blurry, he was too far away. But why would he be lurking at a distance at Casey's funeral? I mean, *we* were doing exactly that, but what was he up to?

CHAPTER 20

"There you are," Lisa said, jogging up behind us. "I thought you might be waiting by the gate but I just followed the smell of Junior Mints. They're on sale at Walgreens, I picked up a box last night."

"Tess is keen on seeing who that guy is," Lena explained, pointing towards the figure still lurking behind the tree closest to the funeral party. We were *also* lurking behind a tree; Kathleen had insisted on a slow approach in case the guy was 'packing heat'.

Having my glasses on meant that I was able to see the ghosts floating around the place in great detail. It was distracting to say the least.

"Is he a vampire?" Lisa asked.

"If he is he should be very afraid!" Kathleen said, making her voice louder towards the end of the sentence and prompting a few of the mourners to turn their heads. Gran was shaking her head in disappointment as the four of us leapt back behind the tree trunk to hide from prying eyes.

"Kat, move!" Michelle barked.

"Why? I'm in camouflage. They can't see me!"

"You are only wearing camouflage trousers. What about your skin? Your white t-shirt? Your shotgun? You're hardly inconspicuous."

"Hey, what's going on back there?" a voice yelled. Michelle swore under her breath and as the voice spoke again I knew why, "I can see you!" It was Steve.

"Oh, hey Steve," Michelle said, stepping out so that he could see her.

"Why are you hiding back here?" he asked. "Wh- why does she have a gun?"

"There's a killer on the loose, one that you have yet to apprehend. It's for self-protection," Michelle answered.

"Best way to stay safe is probably to put *her* behind bars then, wouldn't you say?" He was pointing at me. Clearly we were all as bad at hiding as Kathleen. My eyes darted back toward the tree where the figure had been stood, he was looking our way now and I could see his face clearly. Bobby.

"What about him?" I said. Well, *shouted.* More and more eyes were aimed our way and I could feel another hot flush coming on. Or was it just the regular bout of heat you feel when you've become the unexpected center of attention?

"Bobby? What about him?" Steve asked.

"Hey!" I yelled, stepping away from the tree and closing the gap between Bobby and me. "Where were you Saturday night?"

"He already gave me his alibi, he doesn't owe you an explanation," Steve called.

"Will you shut your stupid face for five seconds?" Michelle barked.

"I went for a walk to the island," Bobby replied.

"So you didn't go to the engagement party?" I asked. "You weren't there arguing with your ex-fiancé in the alley behind the bar?"

"What are you doing here, Tess?" Jack yelled. "Come to gloat?" He stepped out of the crowd in a black suit with a look on his face that made it clear I wasn't welcome.

"Did you know that Casey was engaged before? That she cheated on this guy with you?"

"Cheated? That ended years ago, she said—"

"It was last year," Bobby interrupted. "You're engagement party was booked for the same date that we were due to get married." *Oh.*

"I asked you a question," I repeated.

"I didn't argue with Casey outside the bar, alright," Bobby replied. "I don't know what you're talking about."

"I do…" Liam said, stepping forward. I remembered my dad saying he'd seen Liam and Casey in the parking lot on Saturday through a window. Jack grabbed Liam's suit jacket, scrunching the lapels in his fists.

"Did you kill her?" Jack yelled.

"No! No, I would never!" Liam screeched, trying to break himself loose from Jacks grip. "We argued a little, then I asked if she could give me a ride to work."

"What?" Jack snapped.

"You didn't have a shift on Saturday night," Louise said, joining our little group from behind.

Jack's knuckles whitened as he gripped tighter, "liar."

"I just wanted to talk, I didn't have a shift, no, but my house is super close to Shaded Wood so I could walk home from there," Liam said.

"But you've been getting rides from Casey for weeks," I added. "If you could walk there so easily then… *ah.* You were trying to build up the courage to say something. Right? Looking for excuses to be alone."

"My car isn't broken," he admitted. "But she was marrying this psychopath and we stopped hanging out like we used to. I didn't kill her though. I swear. Let go of me!"

"So she drove you to work, then what?" Michelle pressed.

"Can you get him off me?" Liam said. Jack reluctantly let go, but he kept his hands balled into fists as if ready to punch someone at a moment's notice. "I thanked her for the ride, then pretended to go into the building. That's it. I walked around the front as if I was gonna head through reception and then I just went home. People saw me, the guy who owns my building saw me, one of my neighbors came round to ask me if I'd seen her missing cat at one point. I went home and stayed home. I swear."

"What were you arguing about?" I asked.

"She picks the wrong guy. She always picks the wrong guy. How am I supposed to watch her get married to a guy that pushed her down the stairs?"

"She fell," Jack snapped.

"Did she now?" Liam snarled.

"I never lay a finger on her, I swear. She fell, and I took her to get checked out immediately. We would argue, I would shout... I never hurt her."

"Her car was still there," I said. "She drove you to Shaded Wood and then what? Why didn't she drive back to the party? Where did she go?"

"I don't know," Liam shrugged. Jack swung for Liam, who managed to duck at the last minute but quickly stood back up again to throw a punch at Jack's jaw. I half-considered saying something to break up the fight but at that point it was a 'not my circus, not my monkeys' situation and I figured they should work it out between themselves like the adults there were supposed to be.

"Hey, where's Bobby?" I asked, looking back at the tree he had been stood next to and finding him gone. That couldn't be a good sign. "Steve, Michelle said Bobby had an alibi, that you verified it."

"That's true," Steve replied.

"What was the alibi?"

"None of your business, that's what."

"Steve, I swear to god—" Michelle snapped, flicking his right ear. "Where was he on Saturday night?"

"Kettle Island," Steve said, rubbing the side of his head. "He was on the island from five thirty to around ten. There's CCTV of him walking along Bridge Street towards his house at ten fifteen."

"You really are an idiot, Steve," I huffed.

"What?"

"The tide was high from eight. Kettle Bridge was underwater hours before it was scheduled to be. There's no way that Bobby walked off that island at ten o'clock. And now he's taken off, probably because he killed Casey and realized we were about to figure that out."

"You really are an idiot, Steve," Michelle added.

"When you said you checked his alibi, what did that involve?" I asked.

"I checked the cameras! I mean… I thought you killed Casey; it seemed like a real waste of time for me to be digging through tidal charts or whatever," Steve shrugged.

"A swell wouldn't show up on a tidal chart, the whole point was that it happened unexpectedly!"

"You're about to feel foolish because a swell is actually—"

"Shut up, Steve!" Michelle and Lena shouted in unison.

"He followed me," Liam yelled, throwing Jack off him and scrambling to his feet with a busted lip and a torn jacket. "When I went to the hotel with your dad, he was outside. When my shift ended Louise sent someone to take over and so I left, Casey had offered to drive me home again so I was walking back to Shaded Wood and Bobby was waiting in the parking lot when I got there. I don't know if he knew I saw him, he took off before I could say anything."

"You didn't think to bring this up until now?" I huffed.

"No one spoke to me," Liam replied, looking over at Steve. "I figured you would come and ask me questions, but no one did. Louise already told him to stay away from the home, he stopped coming into the building and would just be outside. I told *him* about it, but you said he had—"

"That he had been cleared," Steve said, finishing Liam's sentence. He slowly turned to Michelle who was giving him a look that could curdle milk, "so this looks bad, admittedly there have been some oversights on my part, but what I would like to point out is—"

"I'm going to deal with you later," Michelle said, leaning closer to him and narrowing her eyes, "I haven't decided what I'm going to do yet, but you won't like it. I can tell you that much."

"Okay, there's only so far that boy can get on foot. I say we split, cover more ground," Kathleen began. "Remember, rats are good at hiding. If you want to catch a rat, think like a rat."

"Tess, you're with me," Michelle said, grabbing my arm and tugging. I followed her lead and hurried across the grass, my shoes sinking into the soft ground and making my ankle ache in protest of the uneven surface. Behind us I could see the rest of the 'book club' splitting into pairs and setting off on a man hunt. Jack was now back on his feet and brushing himself off, his whereabouts for an hour and a half of Saturday night still unaccounted for.

"Has this graveyard always been so big?" It was populated with hundreds upon hundreds of tombstones, statues, and trees. There wasn't a straight line of sight in any direction. A huge Willow tree sprawled across the sky, casting shadow over a vast area of greenery. There was a wooded area, undisturbed and untamed by the people that maintain the land.

"It's for wildlife," Michelle said, answering the question before I'd asked it. "They have to leave some parts like that, some environmental initiative. The whole town is built alongside a national park, but apparently the mice and whatever need a couple of hundred square feet over here, too."

"Mice and *rats*, right?"

"You think he's in there?"

Through my glasses I could see the floating figure of a woman approaching with a mischievous look on her face, "any chance you've misplaced a man that won't stop crying? He's very loud."

"Oh, yes, he's with us," I replied. "Thanks MJ."

"How do you know my name?"

"Call it a hunch," I said. "Michelle, he's in there."

"It seems unfair that you have been a witch for three days and have already got some sort of ghost intel network," she mumbled as we moved forward. Beneath the trees it was dark, much darker than I had anticipated given how bright the sky was. The tree canopy was impenetrable which was no doubt why Bobby had chosen this as his hiding place.

Somewhere in the distance I could hear Kathleen's voice yelling about something or other, and the sound of cars starting. People were done with Casey's funeral – and the spectacle of watching three men that had been in love with her try to fight to the death. Bobby hadn't fought. He'd just run away. Each step into the wooded area took us further from daylight, even with my glasses on I was barely able to make out the shapes in the shadows.

I clutched my bag a little tighter, wishing I *had* brought a weapon like Kathleen had suggested. I stopped moving for a second and listened, expecting to hear my sister's footsteps or breath. Nothing. She wasn't there. This was not a good time for me to have lost my backup.

Movement.

Cracking branches under bodyweight, but not from the path I'd just followed. It was coming from in front of me, someone was moving my way. I squinted in the dark, trying to focus on anything that looked like a human silhouette. A whisp of smoke. MJ reappeared at my side and whispered, "get him!"

Something struck me, hard and heavy against the side of my head. It knocked me off my feet and I landed palms down on the ground. I felt sharp stones slice into my hands, branches scratching at my arms. I reached into my pocket to grab a fistful of salt and threw it into Bobby's face. He shrieked, frantically rubbing at his eyes to alleviate the stinging blindness he was experiencing. I rolled onto my knees and then onto my feet.

In the dim light I could see tears streaming down his cheeks as his eyes tried to flush the salt away. "It was an accident," he said.

"You accidentally waited outside in the parking lot of where she works, strangled her, and then carried her over to the pool of my hotel to try and hide what you'd done?"

"It wasn't suppose to happen like that," he sniffed, his eyes now open and locked onto me. In the moment that he lunged at me, I swung my purse at his face. I don't have a great amount of fighting experience, any time a patient got violent at the hospital I would have a dozen staff by my side in an instant and I never really had to deal with it. What I *did* know was that if you have a bag filled with two giant, heavy water bottles and you smash someone in the face with it that they will be knocked off balance.

What I also knew was that once you've knocked them off balance, you can easily kick them in the crotch and run for your life while the police surround the wooded area and start to work their way inward. I kicked, turned, and ran.

As I collapsed onto the grass in the sunlight, I watched Bobby be dragged toward a police car that had driven up to the trees where I'd found him. Michelle had called it in, turned around expecting to see me, and realized I'd gone in alone. Jack was stood by the patrol car and even from here I could see him looking at me.

He'd thought I'd killed Casey, and I thought he might have done it. It's quite common for people to vilify each other after a divorce like the one we went through, but maybe we'd both taken things a little far. I watched the rest of the 'book club' approaching from across the graveyard and felt relieved that my *real* back up had finally arrived.

CHAPTER 21

The reception area was pristine. I had made sure that the staff were aware that this area of the hotel was how we, as a business, made a first impression to our guests and for the two nights that we'd been open they had kept the place up to my standards.

I sat behind the reception desk and enjoyed the sound of guests eating their breakfasts down the hall, muffled conversations and laughter. I'd worried I wouldn't get to this moment. The last week and a half had been as physically exhausting as it had been mentally.

One couple had checked out already, and I had more checking in later that afternoon. Tourists excited about a stay in a seaside town were flocking to the website as I'd set *dangerously* generous prices for the rooms to get the ball rolling.

It certainly helped that the newspapers had run a story with a press statement from the Kettle Harbor police department stating that they had a suspect in custody that had signed a confession regarding the murder of Casey Quinn. The fact that the Moody Moon hotel was the place where her body had been found didn't seem to deter guests as much as I'd thought it would. Was it possible that out-of-towners hadn't run a google search before they booked? Sure. I certainly wasn't going to bring it up if they didn't, though.

Molly, Lena's niece, came in to begin her shift on the reception desk and I looked at the clock with surprise; I hadn't even realized my shift was due to end. Not that my shift ever really truly ended, it just meant I could do work at my kitchen table instead of in the hotel. "It's a beautiful day out there," Molly said, "I ran here along Bridge Street and the water is so calm. Are you running again now?"

I looked at her sweat-free face, the perfect skin of a twenty-year-old woman that doesn't turn beetroot red when walking up a flight of stairs. "I'm getting back into it, slowly," I replied. The last run I'd been on was when I got the text from Michelle telling me to hurry over to the hotel. Maybe it was time to put my sneakers back on and get back into the habit. "Two rooms checked out already, just waiting on room ten but they still have half an hour," I explained.

"Got it," Molly nodded, "in twenty-nine minutes I'll be outside their door banging pans together."

"Or you could walk around the outside of the building and scream through their window, I'll leave it up to you," I laughed. I stood up, my legs ached from having been sat down for such a long time and I tried to suppress the urge to make a groaning noise in front of Molly. Getting out of chairs was often accompanied by some sort of grunt now, and I didn't want to show my age in front of company.

"Have you got big plans for the day?" she asked.

"Just headed over to see my dad, paying a fine so that my car gets released from the tow yard, and that's about it," I shrugged. "Oh, there's a guy coming this afternoon to set up the security camera for the pool area. He's replacing the back gate lock and he's bringing a few copies of the keys for us."

Based on Bobby's confession, it seemed that he had shoulder charged the back gate and managed to gain access. I *had* locked up after the launch party, but the lock was old and the screws were loose enough that it wasn't hard to break in. He'd been visiting his grandmother and spotted Casey's car pull into the lot. He said that Liam took off towards the building but that Casey leaned against the hood of her car for a few minutes – which is when he approached her.

Apparently there were only so many rejections that Bobby could handle before he snapped, and given that it was the date on which they were supposed to get married his mental health was already hanging on by a thread. She cheated on him, broken his heart, and then moved on painfully quickly. He strangled her in the parking lot then panicked, scooped her up and ran to the hotel.

He claims that he was looking for me because he knew I'd been a nurse, he wanted my help to save her. I call bull on that one. Why not go into Shaded Wood and ask one of the health professionals in there? Why not call for an ambulance and stay put? It's one thing to kill a person, it's a whole other thing to try and cover up what you've done. Michelle is confident that he will be staring at the inside of a prison cell for a very long time.

I walked towards the doors that lead out to the pool area and watched Casey laying out on one of the sun loungers, her ghost shimmering under the golden light beaming down at her. I'd told her what we'd learned about how she died, she'd been horrified by it, and still had no memories of her own about the event. Gran said they would come to her eventually and I took her word for it, given that she was a ghost herself.

Casey was able to confirm one detail, though. Jack hadn't pushed her down the stairs, they'd been arguing in their bedroom – *my* old bedroom, but I didn't interrupt her – and she'd tried to walk away and slipped. Jack had tried to grab her arm to stop her from falling but was unsuccessful. He was still a terrible person, there was no getting away from that, but at least he wasn't going around attacking his own girlfriend. Not physically, anyway.

The bloodied knuckles and the scratches on Jack? The missing hour and a half from his evening? The missed call I had from him on my phone? All connected. He'd drunk enough at his engagement party that he thought it was a good idea to stop in at my house for a visit, only I wasn't there. My own timeline for the night was unclear, so maybe I *was* home but slept through the calls and the pounding on my door.

He'd told Steve about it, who then told Michelle, who then passed it along to me. He'd punched the front door because he thought I was ignoring him, then *something* had scratched at his face and caught his neck. I suspected that the *something* was in fact my grandmother.

He hadn't left a voicemail, and there was no way I was going to seek him out to ask him about it, so maybe I'd never know why he had darkened my door that night.

I walked out of the front doors of Moody Moon and started off down the street towards the Shaded Wood care home at a brisk pace. Molly had been right; it was beautiful out here today. In the distance I could see a Whale Watch boat out on a tourist trip, the tide was low enough for Kettle Bridge to be exposed and people were crossing over to the island for a quick stroll.

The surprise high tide on Saturday night that busted Bobby's alibi was my doing. It was connected to my use of magic; I'd passed out and woken up at home and that burst of power had messed with the water around the island. If I hadn't done that then maybe I never would have figured out who'd killed Casey, so in a way I was *glad* Gran had shown up and scared me half to death. But don't tell *her* that.

Inside the day room I could see my dad sat by the TV with a few other residents, Louise on the phone arguing with somebody that would regret calling in the first place, and Chris. He smiled when he saw me, and I felt my fingers get warm as if magic was about to erupt from them. I quickly balled my hands into fists and walked over to him, catching Lionel's bare backside streaking across the lawn outside as I did so.

"He's naked again," I said, gesturing to the window.

"Louise suggested we stop giving him attention for it, as if that might encourage him to stop. So far it had not made a difference," he explained, turning to watch a naked old man doing cartwheels across the grass. He was facing the building when he did them, which meant that we saw *everything* tumble around as he performed his little gymnastics routine. That's when I saw a white light behind him.

I reached into my bag and pulled out my glasses to bring the light into detail, MJ. She'd found him. I don't know if bumping into me in the graveyard had somehow made this happen, but I was glad it had worked out. Even from here I could see that she was laughing, and I thought about everything Lionel had said to me last week.

"How's the hotel?" Chris asked.

"I want you to have my phone number," I blurted. He smiled, and behind him I saw my dad turn at the sound of my voice. "I like talking to you, and you like talking to me, and I want to do more of it."

"Okay," he said, pulling his cell phone and handing it to me so I could type in my number. Once I handed it back, he pressed a few buttons rapidly and then my phone buzzed in my pocket. He'd sent me a text message so that I had his number too. His message had two words, 'nice glasses'.

"Now I can keep you updated on the plant you gave me; I usually can't keep green things alive because I either forget to water them or *over* water them, but this one still looks good after a week in my bedroom," I said.

"I'd love to see it," he smiled, then realized what he'd said. "Not your bedroom, I meant— just that you said you'd put it in your room and— I'm not trying to invite myself to—"

I reached to grab his hand and squeezed it, just like I had on Bridge Street when he'd said I was beautiful. It only then that I noticed something, he'd taken off his wedding ring. There was still a tan line to show where it had been, but the ring itself was gone. "You took it off?"

"It was time," he smiled. I felt the heat in my cheeks, and I could swear I was floating an inch off the ground, but it just felt that way because I free of the weight of everything that had been loaded onto me the past year. "I need to confess something."

"What?"

"I gave you a fake plant. You don't need to water it at all, it will just keep looking like that no matter what you do," he said.

"Well that's embarrassing," I laughed. "For me, I mean. I was feeling proud of myself for finally looking after something properly and it was plastic all along. The fake ones they make now are so realistic! I wonder if I ever would have noticed."

"I'm sure you would have eventually," he smiled. "So because I have some family in town, I could probably get some free childcare tonight. Maybe we could grab dinner somewhere?"

"Sounds good to me. I can't be out too late; I have a book club thing."

"I didn't know you were in a book club. You are full of surprises."

"You have no idea," I replied, my mind wandering to the group of witches I would be hanging out with at Books and Such. This week Kathleen had once again been in charge of selecting the book for us all to read, another raunchy vampire romance novel that was definitely aimed at an adult audience. I asked Michelle when someone else would have a turn to choose the book and she said that they picked names out of a hat but *somehow* Kathleen's name was selected seventy percent of the time.

"I've got one more session today and then I'll go home and sort out someone to take care of Ruby. I'll text you!" he said, letting go of my hand after one final squeeze and turning down a corridor. We'd talked about taking it slow and we both had a ton of emotional baggage on our shoulders, but I couldn't stop smiling. I was smitten.

I walked over to my dad and sat in a chair beside him, the smile on my face still enormous. Dad smiled back at me, no doubt he'd overheard much of the conversation.

"Don't give me that look," I laughed. He shrugged. "You know I actually took some advice from Lionel, would you believe it? He's wiser than you'd think."

Of course at that very moment Lionel streaked past the closest window.

"Yeah, he's a real intellectual," I added. "Hey, I heard a rumor that you won a fruit cake at bingo the other day. Did you save me a slice?"

He gestured to the nurse's station and I knew he meant he'd asked Louise to keep it in her little refrigerator. Fruit cake theft was a real problem around here, so all precautions had to be taken. I walked over to the desk, pointed at the fridge door and Louise retrieved a saran wrapped plate for me. She was still yelling down the phone but it was cordless so she could wander.

By the time I returned to the chair the other residents had

wandered away, meaning that the two of us had an element of privacy.

"Hey, I have a question. How did you find out about mom having powers? When did she tell you? I don't want to feel like I'm keeping secrets but at the same time I don't want to send him running for the hills. Ooo – walnuts!" I took a huge bite of cake and looked at my dad who pointed at me, then tapped his head. *What's really on your mind?*

"If I'd told any of this to Jack he would have lost it. I mean, classic narcissist behavior in a way, right? The thought that he wasn't the most powerful one in a relationship would just eat him up. I don't get the impression Chris is like that, but he's had his own fair share of heartbreak—"

"You'll be fine," dad said.

I almost choked on fruit cake. He had just spoken to me. Out loud. I'd heard it. I'd seen his lips move and he had said words.

"Did you—?"

I put the plate down on the table beside me and threw my arms around him. I didn't know if it would ever happen, but after months of silence I'd finally heard his voice again.

"Not so tight, Tess," he laughed.

"How is this happening?" I said, releasing him so that I could lean back enough to see his face. He shrugged. "Have you been working on this with the speech and language woman? I thought you weren't getting anywhere with that, I didn't think you—"

"Slow and steady," he replied.

"Michelle is going to have an aneurism when I tell her. Wait, I should call her right now and put you on!"

I started dialing her number excitedly with my trembling fingers, I couldn't wait for her to hear this. I'd been talking to dad without a reply for months and months, all of the experiences I'd had with Gran's ghost, with witchcraft, all of it had happened when he couldn't answer me fully. But now? Now it was time to start asking some real questions.

THANKS FOR READING

Thanks for reading, I hope you enjoyed the book.

It would really help me out if you could leave an honest review with your thoughts and rating on Amazon.

Every bit of feedback helps!

ALSO BY MARA WEBB

~ **Ongoing** ~

Hallow Haven Witch Mysteries

An English Enchantment

Compass Cove Cozy Mysteries

~ **Completed** ~

Wicked Witches of Pendle Island

Wildes Witches Mysteries

Raven Bay Mysteries

Wicked Witches of Vanish Valley

MAILING LIST

Want to be notified when I release my latest book? Join my mailing list. It's for new releases only. No spam:

Click here to join!

I'll also send you a free 120,000 word book as a thank you for signing up.

marawebbauthor.com

amazon.com/-/e/B081X754NL
facebook.com/marawebbauthor
twitter.com/marawebbauthor
bookbub.com/authors/mara-webb

www.ingramcontent.com/pod-product-compliance
Lightning Source LLC
Chambersburg PA
CBHW061427160726
47995CB00003B/787